THE
SPECI

This book is dedicated to the rescue dogs,
their trainers and their handlers all over the world.

CHAPTER ONE

DANICA FIELDING tucked her legs up under her in the white wicker rocking chair, and pulled the patchwork lap quilt up to her waist. It was warm for April, with a nice breeze blowing in from the river, so she didn't need the quilt for warmth. It had become her habit these past sixteen months, though. More a security blanket than anything else. When she felt alone or tired or melancholy, out came the quilt as a comforter. It was amazing how good it felt to be tucked underneath it.

Shutting her eyes and leaning her head back against the chair, she drew in a long, deep breath, then let it out slowly. It was good to be here by herself. After so many months of attention and people fussing all over her…first from the doctors and medical staff in the Brazil hospital, then the rehab attendants in the Texas facility, followed by family and friends huddling around when she'd finally returned to her tiny apartment in Dallas…there hadn't really been an hour in her waking day since the accident when she'd been alone. They all kept watch over her, fretting over every one of her aches and pains, and she loved them for that. But she needed this time away. Time to be by herself, to think about her future, to find her way back to her life, to figure out what came next. To begin healing from all the emotional wounds. It was bound to happen.

Physically, she was coming along splendidly, according to her doctors. Physical therapy was over with now. No more walkers and crutches and canes. She'd progressed through the succession and finally come away with barely a limp. That after so many surgeries. So now it was up to her to keep her daily exercises going and further her progress, build up more strength and endurance. Which she was doing. Faithfully.

But emotionally? It still hurt so badly because she hadn't had time to deal with the grimmest aspects of her accident, except in the dark hours of the night when people left her alone to sleep. Which was precisely when she didn't want to deal with the horrors of what had happened because the images were so vivid then. Even now, she could still see herself so clearly, going up the mountainside with Tom, looking for survivors in that old wooden schoolhouse in the mudslide. Tom trying to find a way in from one side while she was trying from another…then the building collapsing on her.

Now, nine surgeries and all those months of physical therapy behind her, she didn't want any of that coming back to her in the dark. Which was why did didn't sleep much at night. It was better to leave on the lights and prowl, or read. Then come out onto her porch and doze through the light of the morning, when she was so exhausted that thoughts and dreams that otherwise might have come during the night would not.

Thoughts and dreams of Tom.

A lump still formed in her throat when she thought about him. She had cared so much for him, and rumors among her rescue colleagues in Global Response had had her marrying Tom sometime in the future. Marriage and babies… Perhaps she might have, even though, at the time, she and Tom had never talked seriously about it because their relationship hadn't gotten quite to that point. It had still been new, feelings definitely growing between them, although not to the extent that they had been planning the future. It had all been ahead of them, though. Only now she would never know how it might have worked out. And thinking about Tom as she did so often, and trying to visualize the life she had missed with him, her heart ached. She'd been falling in love with tall, handsome, athletic Tom McCain and his death was one of the reasons she still hid herself under the patchwork quilt her grandmother had made for her years ago. That quilt protected her from all the things that never would be.

Tom had died too young. But he'd died a hero, saving the life of a little girl. Dani did take some comfort in that, especially during those long, dark hours when she crept about her house trying not to think. Even so, that still didn't ease all the pain.

"Morning, Danica," a chipper voice called to her from the sidewalk.

Nice voice, sexy voice, but one she didn't want to hear. Since she'd come home to stay at her grandmother's old house several weeks ago, Dr. Cameron Enderlein had taken it upon himself to look out after her. Or, at least, that's what he thought he was doing. He was a handsome man, but so annoying to her at a time when she didn't want interference or chipper good mornings or sexy voices in her life. It was too soon. Even after all these months, it was still too soon.

Instead of answering the good doctor, Dani kept her eyes shut, hoping he would think her asleep and simply walk on by. That's what she usually did when he came this way on his morning strolls, and it always worked. She'd shut her eyes, think about…well, *him*. She didn't want to but that's who popped into her mind at odd moments, probably because she was so intent on keeping him out. No such luck right now, though. He was not only wheedling his way into her thoughts, but from the sound of her squeaky gate opening and closing, he was, most likely, wandering his way up her walk.

"I was in the neighborhood," he started.

Dani still didn't open her eyes in the desperate hope that her little deception would fool him, but she was the one who was being fooled because the closer he got to her the better she could picture him in her mind. Good-looking for sure, probably two or three years older than her. Aggravatingly bright smile. And she was fighting herself now to keep from taking a quick peek.

Except she just didn't want anything bright in her life now. Cameron Enderlein might be a perfectly nice man, but she wasn't ready to do anything more than sitting, observing, thinking. And letting the days seep slowly into her pores and push out just a bit more of the tragedy each and every time. So rather than standing to greet Dr. Enderlein, or even being polite enough to say hello, Dani merely kept her eyes shut as she heard his footsteps on the pavement getting closer and closer.

"Thought I'd check in and see how you're doing."

She didn't answer.

"You look good. Maybe a little pale, but overall good."

Now he was diagnosing her? She was tempted to open her eyes enough to catch a glimpse of that infuriatingly gorgeous smile on him, but she didn't. Rather, she continued to ignore him, hoping he would leave her alone. A futile hope, most likely, since she didn't hear his footsteps walking away.

"Beautiful morning," he said after a long pause, not to be deterred by her attempts to put him off. "Nice day for a walk. Do you do that, Danica? Get out and walk? Exercise at all? Take an opportunity to see how lovely it is out here?"

This was becoming ridiculous. It seemed the longer she ignored him, the more he was intent upon staying there, trying to get her to notice him.

"Temperature's just right," he continued. "Not too warm, not too chilly."

She almost wanted to laugh at his feeble attempt. In fact, it was all she could do to keep herself from smiling over the way he was trying to get a rise out of her. Persistence was a good trait and she almost liked his. Almost.

"Air's nice and fresh. The river's looking particularly pristine."

The man simply didn't stop, and she had an idea he wouldn't until she spoke. So, in the interests of getting him to go away, she did finally speak. "I'm doing fine, Doctor," she said stiffly, her eyes still closed. "Getting sufficient exercise, walking when the mood hits, enjoying the temperature, pleased about the river's pristine conditions. And at present I'm trying to enjoy the *solitude* of the morning." Not that Dr. Enderlein would take the hint. He never did. Three weeks of his advances and her ignoring every last one of them, yet he still didn't get it. She didn't want to be bothered—not by him, not by anyone. *Leave Danica Fielding alone.* Everyone else in town seemed to respect that unspoken law governing her life now, so why wouldn't he? "Thank you for stopping by, Doctor. I appreciate your concern, but now, if you'll excuse me, I have several things to attend to in the house." She finally opened her eyes and started to push herself forward in her chair, not really wanting to get up but hoping that he would be polite about this and simply go away, since that's practically what she'd just asked him to do.

"Are you due for a physical or something?" he asked, totally out of the blue. "Any kind of medical services? You've been here three weeks now, and so far you haven't come to my office. So I thought…"

"I beg your pardon?" She looked straight at him, her eyes flashing with indignation. "You thought I'd be requiring a physical exam performed *by you?* What makes you think I'd allow *you* to do it?" She snorted her disdain. Dr. Enderlein was a handsome man and, yes, when he walked away from her on his morning strolls she did enjoy the view—she still had *some* normal urges left after all. But what in the world gave him the right to come to her door, peddling his medical wares? Honestly, the man bothered her. She didn't hate him or anything like that. She just didn't want him here in any capacity, professional, personal or otherwise.

"Actually, I didn't think you would. But I did get a nice rise out of you, didn't I?" He smiled. "Coaxed a little conversation."

"A rise? You got a rise out of me?" He'd baited her and succeeded. She did have to hand it to him. His persistence had paid off. "That's not a rise, Doctor, neither is it conversation. I'm merely responding to an…intrusion. Trying to be polite without pointing to the gate and asking you to be careful not to slam it on the way out."

Dani finally gave in to temptation and gave him a good, hard look, head to toe then back up again, stopping at his eyes and turning a dry glare on him. Tall, beautiful hair—dark brown and wavy, neatly clipped but a little over his collar. He would have been her type once, maybe even more than Tom had been. And she couldn't—not look, not touch, not anything! Without meaning to, though, she did glance at his ring finger and saw what she'd expected to see there—nothing. Dr. Cameron Enderlein was a single man, according to her grandmother. "And trying to be polite about telling you that my physical condition is none of your business, and if I require a doctor, it won't be you."

"Polite?" He chuckled.

"I could have said something to the effect that I wouldn't see you if you were the last doctor on the face of the earth, but I didn't, so that *was* being polite." Dr. Enderlein practiced part-time medicine, and it was a pity Lexington hadn't been fortunate enough to snag a full-timer with a little more dedication. But they hadn't. They'd gotten Dr. Enderlein instead and as far as she was concerned, she didn't want any of those twenty hours a week that he worked. Nothing personal. He seemed fine enough, and she'd heard good things. In general, people liked him. But he just wasn't what she was looking for. No particular reason, except perhaps…his eyes. Beautiful, soulful eyes. Eyes that took one look and knew. She didn't want to think of her physician in terms of having beautiful eyes or…a nice physique. Damn, where had *that* come from?

Dani blinked, trying to push those wandering thoughts aside. They'd popped up about Cameron Enderlein before and she'd reasoned them away by calling it a drastic overreaction to being lonely, being without a man, missing Tom. "Like I said, don't slam the gate too hard on your way out." Dani shifted back in the chair, pulling the quilt even higher.

Instead of arguing with her as she expected he would do, Cameron gave her a lazy smile, and held out a small white paper bag. "Care to share breakfast with me before I go? Nothing better than a cinnamon bun from Carston's Bakery."

She did love Nora Carston's cinnamon buns better than almost anything else in the world. But not this morning, and not with this man. "Not hungry," she said, which was true. She wasn't. In fact, she couldn't remember the last time she'd actually been hungry.

"I could fix us a cup of tea to go with them," he suggested. "I'm assuming you have tea here?"

"Exactly why do you think I want to have breakfast with you, Doctor? When have I ever given you the impression I want to do *anything* with you?"

Even though she'd snapped at him, it didn't faze him. He still smiled, still held out the cinnamon buns. "Actually, I have no impression that you do want to have breakfast with me. But when I stopped at the bakery a little while ago and bought a cinnamon bun for myself, Nora Carston asked if I would be coming out this way. When I told her I would, she asked me to bring one to you. Which is what I'm doing. And I thought that as we each have a cinnamon bun, neither of which are connected to the other in any way other than by coincidence since I did not purchase yours, we might eat them together while they're still warm."

The man had an answer for everything. Yesterday, Daniel Rutgers, who owned the magazine stand on Main Street, had given Dr. Enderlein the daily newspaper to bring to her. The day before that, Gemma Gannon had sent oranges from her fruit stand. It was a town conspiracy, and Cameron Enderlein seemed to be the popular errand boy. Until now, though, he'd dropped his offerings at her mail box and continued on his way. Which was the way she'd preferred it. No relationship, no conversation. But now he was opening the door to those things, and she didn't like it one little bit. "Look, Dr. Enderlein—"

"Cameron," he interrupted. "Call me Cameron."

That would make them friends, which she didn't want to be. "Look, *Dr. Enderlein,*" she persisted, "I appreciate the concern, and I'm trying not to seem too ungracious about this. But I didn't come to Lexington to socialize with the people here. Not yet, anyway. I know everybody is worried about me but I want to be alone. *Alone.*"

Instead of being put off, Cameron Enderlein actually walked up the six wooden steps to the porch and put the bag of cinnamon buns down on the table next to Dani, then simply stood there and stared down at her. Vivid eyes, quirky smile, he just didn't give up. "Are you still on any medication?" he asked, quite matter-of-factly.

"That's none of your business," she snapped.

"As your doctor…"

"Get this through your head, Doctor. *You are not my doctor.* Not now, not ever."

"Then call me Cameron."

"I would, but then you'd take it to mean I want to be your

friend, which I don't." She had enough friends. Too many. It hurt when they died. Caused pain that wouldn't quit. "I don't want to be bothered by you, I don't want to be friends with you, and I don't want your damned cinnamon buns. Do you understand me, Doctor? Go away! Don't come back!" She couldn't be any more plain about it than that. Him being here was an intrusion, and it reminded her of all the things she didn't want to be reminded of.

"So, no tea?" he asked, the smile still not faded from his face.

"Don't you ever give up?" Dani dropped her head back against the chair and shut her eyes. The man was obtuse. Nothing got through. In one form or another they'd done this almost every day since she'd been here, and it didn't matter how often she sent him away. He still came back, still bothered her.

"Do *you* ever give up, Danica?" he asked, his voice so deep and sexy it caused goose-bumps to rise on her arms.

She rubbed at her arms, trying to brush away her reaction to him. "Look, I've got a little money saved up. Could I just bribe you to go away and leave me alone?"

He cocked a playful eyebrow. "So the lady has a sense of humor."

She opened one eye and looked up at him. "The lady has no sense of humor whatsoever. I'm serious about bribing you to go away." Then she shut her eye.

Cameron laughed out loud. "When I was in medical school, I did well. Top of my class. My instructors said it wasn't because I was a better student than anyone else so much as it was that I was more persistent. When all else failed, I just plowed on through. Didn't give up."

"You call that persistent? Don't you mean stubborn?" she asked, opening both eyes this time.

"Depends on your definition, I suppose. On me, I like persistent. On you, I think stubborn fits better."

"So now you're going to insult me?" Actually, she wasn't insulted. Another time, another place, she might have enjoyed this little back and forth conversation with him because, under normal circumstances, she did like a sparky little tiff. She might have even caught herself liking Dr. Enderlein. But not now, not in a personal way. That part of her life was still too raw and liking somebody, and enjoying their company, made you too vulnerable. She didn't want to be vulnerable any more. It hurt too much. Being lonely hurt so much, too, but right now that was her choice. Vulnerable and lonely were such a dismal pair, though.

"Insults go better over a cup of tea and a nice cinnamon bun, don't you think?"

"If I give in to this, if I allow you to eat your breakfast here, will you go away and never come back?" In a way, she hoped he'd refuse. As much as she didn't want him here, she wasn't nearly as bothered as she was letting on. Perhaps the bother was just a pretense, something that seemed right under the circumstances? Something that seemed loyal to Tom? Didn't matter, though, because while her intellect was telling her one thing, trying to rationalize the situation, her emotions still ruled the moment.

"Never is such a long time. I can't promise you never, but I'm open to making a deal."

In spite of herself, Dani smiled. The man had a way about him. Couldn't deny that! "One week, then. I'll allow you to have tea here, and in return you'll leave me alone for a week. That's your deal, Doctor." One week, and he'd fall out of the habit. Or decide she wasn't worth the time he was wasting on her.

He extended his hand to shake on the deal. "Fine. One week, Danica."

"One week," she said, staring at his hand before she decided to take it. When she did, the smoothness of his skin sent a little tingle skittering up her arm, and she immediately pulled back from him, stunned by her response. Even with Tom she hadn't… Frail nerves, she reasoned. That's all it was. Frail nerves, rocky emotions. "One full week, Doctor."

"Cameron," he corrected.

"The tea is in the kitchen, *Doctor*. I have a breakfast blend in a canister, cups and saucers in the cabinet above the sink, kettle is on the stove. I like mine plain…no sugar, no cream, no lemon. And only moderately hot, not scalding." Once her instructions were finished, she shut her eyes, shifted in her chair, and readjusted her quilt. Then she listened to the screen door slam as Cameron went inside to fix her tea.

"If I could get up and run away, now would be a good time," she said to Dag, her tri-color German shepherd. He was napping lazily on the porch floor next to her chair, totally unconcerned by the whole interchange between her and Cameron Enderlein.

Dag was a rescue dog. He'd saved lives, and now he was relegated to the same useless life she was. It was a pity, wasting such a well-trained animal the way she was, but she couldn't part with him, couldn't give him to Gideon or Priscilla, the other rescue dog handlers on her team. Dag was all she had left, and she loved him. So, like her, he was in retirement, spending his days doing nothing. Of course, she justified that by reminding herself that he hadn't been out on a rescue since the accident, and that he was horribly out of practice. Of course, she was, by profession, a veterinarian, and she knew better. Her dog had natural instincts when it came to rescue work, and it wouldn't take more than a week or two of retraining to get him back to where he used to be.

But selfishly she couldn't do that. She needed Dag. In the dark hours, when she still cried, he was the only one who saw her tears, the only one she wanted to see them. He listened, he comforted. He was all she needed.

Cameron wasn't deluding himself. Having tea with Danica wasn't progress. It was merely a bargain she'd made to get him to go away for awhile. She wasn't being friendly, allowing him to make tea for her like she was. The two of them wouldn't have a cordial chat while they enjoyed their breakfast together. More likely, Danica Fielding would say very little to him. Or nothing at all.

But tomorrow morning, as he took his usual stroll through town, he would have more to report than, "She's doing as well as can be expected." People expected more than that from the only person who braved contact with her. Or, more aptly, provoked contact with her. They stayed away because they didn't know how to approach her, and they were glad for a progress report from him, although he rarely had any progress to give them. Tomorrow would be different, though. He could say they'd had tea together, and people would be thrilled because everybody he'd met in Lexington so far positively adored Dr. Danica Fielding, Doctor of Veterinary Medicine.

He knew the particulars surrounding her accident. People talked, mostly out of concern. They confided fears, so many of which, lately, had been about Danica's recovery. They talked about the accident, the death of a man they'd all thought she would marry, they worried over her injuries, her surgeries, and speculated about her recovery. Good or bad, there weren't many secrets here, and sometimes he felt like an intruder listening in, as people wanted to talk to him about Danica—people including Louise Fielding, Danica's grandmother. She'd given him strict orders to watch over her granddaughter. More intrusion, he supposed, but in a vicarious sense, his concern for Danica was growing like that of everybody else in town. How could it not, the way he heard about her so often?

Cameron sat the copper tea kettle on the old gas stove, turned on the flame, then went into the entry hall to study the photos there on the entry table while the water heated. He knew Danica's life story as well as the details of her accident. Everyone in Lexington had given him a version of her life…from the little girl in pigtails who'd climbed trees to the veterinarian who'd gone out on rescue missions with her dog and saved lives. He studied a photo of her for a moment—high school graduation. She was in a long black robe, holding up her diploma, smiling brightly for the camera. In so many ways, she still looked the same. Short blonde hair, sparkling blue eyes…except that her eyes didn't sparkle now. And the smile he saw in the photo…well, he'd never seen Danica smile. Most of the time when he stopped by on his morning walk, she frowned. Not at him so much as her situation, he thought. She tried to put on a good, blustery front, but he saw through it. Saw through it only too well because it hadn't been that long ago he'd been there himself. Same frowns, same blustery front, same aversions.

Perhaps that's why he was so drawn to her. Certainly, she was a beautiful woman. And in a way he'd had a vicarious relationship with her through the tales of everybody in town. But he knew her deep pain, understood it in ways most people never could. Leukemia had a way of giving you different insights and over the past three years, if he'd learned anything, it was that there were many different ways to survive a tragedy. But one thing that never varied was that it was so damned difficult to survive it alone. Danica was alone. It had been a self-imposed sentence so far. But she was alone, nevertheless. And more than anything, he knew how that felt.

So he watched Danica. Mostly from afar. Except this morning.

Cameron took another look at the graduation photo, and at the smile on the beautiful girl who was about to go out and conquer the world, then he went back to the kitchen to silence the whistling kettle. First he poured his cup, added a little sugar and lemon, then poured Danica's. Plain. Straightforward. Nothing unexpected. As she took her tea, so she lived her life, it seemed.

Except that her life hadn't been very good lately. Which was why he tolerated her unfriendliness. It was simply a matter of her condition. He knew that as well as he knew that, as a girl, she'd won the town spelling competition for five years straight, according to Nora Carston, Raymond McNeely, and Mrs. Blankenship at the grocery store. Only Mrs. Blankenship swore it was six years. Of course, even if he hadn't heard so many glowing accounts of the life of Danica Louise Fielding, all he had to do was look at the photos on her grandmother's hall table to know that the person belonging to the images captured there could never be unfriendly. Not under normal circumstances. Shattered legs, broken pelvis, hysterectomy…those weren't normal circumstances, though.

"Too hot," she said before she'd even touched the tea to her lips.

"It'll cool."

"Which means you'll get to sit here a while longer and wait. Is that why you made it too hot?"

"You give me too much credit, Danica. Heat is one of those relative things. What's hot for one person is only tepid for another."

She looked down at the cinnamon bun he'd placed on a piece of her grandmother's good blue and white china, tempted to take a bite. It looked delicious, smelled delicious, but her stomach was upset, like it was most mornings. Normally, she forced herself to eat a little something by noon, but noon was still a good four hours off, and this cinnamon bun was tempting her in spite of the nausea. "You forced yourself on me, forced your way in my house, so why wouldn't I think you did it on purpose?" She set the bun aside.

"We don't all have ulterior purposes," he said. "Hot tea is hot tea. That's all it is. A minute too long heating in the kettle and you think this is some kind of conspiracy."

"Isn't it?" she asked. "Didn't my grandmother tell you to watch me? Are the people in town pestering you for a report on my condition? Nora Carston gave you this cinnamon bun just to make sure you'll come by and see me, Gemma sends fruit, Daniel sends the newspaper. If that's not a conspiracy, tell me what is."

Cameron laughed as he settled back onto the white wicker loveseat across from Dani's rocking chair. "I'd call it a lot of people who care about you, and don't know how to respond any other way. You're not exactly welcoming them in right now, are you?"

"I came here so I wouldn't have to." Finally, she took a sip of the tea and, admittedly, it was good. Not too strong and bitter, not too weak either. "I've had well over a year of people showing concern every way they knew how, but sometimes you need to be alone. That's where I am now, Doctor. Trying to be alone. I'm sorry it bothers so many people, but I'm almost thirty and I'm really capable of running my life the way I see fit. Even though people, including my grandmother, don't believe that."

She reconsidered the cinnamon bun, pulled off a small bite and ate it. Nausea and all, it was very good.

"Well, you certainly have a beautiful spot here for avoiding people."

That, she did. Her grandmother's white Victorian home with a wrap-around porch, perched on a grassy hill overlooking the Ohio River, sitting far enough from town not to be a part of it but close enough to be convenient, was absolutely perfect—the balm to heal so many ills, she hoped. It was a beautiful spot, a family heirloom, and the place she'd wanted to be for so many months. Of course, her family hadn't been happy about her decision to stay here alone. Her parents had said they would move in with her, her sister had said she would give up her apartment and job in Chicago and move here. Even her grand-mother, who'd been on a waiting list for two years to get her condo in a seniors' community, had said she would sell it and move back. None of which Dani had agreed to, of course. "My great-great-grandfather built it. He owned a barge, traveled back and forth to West Virginia to fetch coal, and he put the house here so my great-great-grandmother would have a good view of him coming down the river."

"A man of impeccable taste," Cameron commented. "If I were to build a house for the lady I loved, this would be the spot."

For a moment, Dani thought about asking him if there was a lady he loved, but she didn't. It was none of her business, and asking such a thing might cause him to think she was interested, or at least interested in being friendly. Which she was not. In another few minutes, he would be gone and she would have her house, and her life, to herself once again. Admittedly, though, she wondered how a man like him had made it so long without marrying. Maybe he had, and divorced. Maybe he was gay. Maybe he lived a life with women coming and going. Whatever the case, as curious as she might be, and she was just a little, she wouldn't ask.

Instead, she merely sipped her tea and ate the remainder of her cinnamon bun. When she was finished, she settled back in her chair, readjusted her quilt, shut her eyes, and waited for Dr. Cameron Enderlein to leave her front porch. And her life.

CHAPTER TWO

DANI tucked the quilt in around her legs, then looked up and down the street below. Another beautiful morning, another perfect day to be outside. It was Dr. Enderlein's usual time to walk by, but he was nowhere to be seen, and Dani stretched forward to look for him. In fact, it had been a week since she'd seen him. Actually, he'd passed by several times, but on the other side of the road, down on the pathway close to the river, and while he hadn't gone so far as to snub her completely, his brief wave of acknowledgment every day from so far away had seemed rather remiss to her. She had, after all, invited him to have tea with her last week.

Well, maybe that was a bit of a stretch. He'd invited himself to fix tea for the two of them, then she'd tolerated him sitting on the porch next to her as he'd drunk his. And, yes, she'd told him to leave her alone for a week after that, which was precisely what he was doing, but Dani hadn't honestly thought he'd take her at her word.

In a way, she was disappointed that he had.

It wasn't like she wanted a friendship with Cameron Enderlein, though, because she didn't. But in her time here he'd become…well, almost like part of her routine. Yes, that was it. He was part of her daily habit, which was why she'd felt the

tiniest twinge of agitation when he hadn't strolled by at his
usual time this morning. Not even on the other side of the road.
"He'd take it the wrong way," she said to Dag, who was napping
on the crocheted rag mat next to the rocker. "If I waved first,
or invited him up for another cup of tea, he'd think that meant
something more than what is between us." Sounded logical,
except she couldn't define what she thought it was between
them other than a wary acquaintance, or two people who might
have been friendly under very different circumstance. "Maybe
he'd think I was looking for a little companionship," she
conceded aloud. "Or a medical shoulder in case I need one."
Which she didn't, *and would not,* but saying it out loud made
it seem reasonable enough.

In truth, there was such an empty spot in her now, and not
just one that had been filled by Tom, but by all of her friends,
especially the ones at Global Response, the crew of search and
rescue experts she'd worked with these past several years. That
whole rescue operation had been a huge part of her life, especially since she'd been the team veterinarian who'd taken care
of the rescue dogs, as well as being a paramedic in her own
right, which had entitled her to participate actively in the
medical needs of the people they rescued. She'd had such a full
life, and now it was gone, which gave her good reason to be
lonely. She missed her work, and she ached every time she
thought about *not* going back to it. But she couldn't. Not after
Tom had been killed. Eventually, she would return to a veterinary practice, because she did love doing that. But she would
not set foot into the rescue field again, in any capacity, because
she'd left her heart for that all smashed to pieces on that
mountain in Brazil where Tom had died.

So now she was lonely.

Perhaps in some way Cameron Enderlein could be a cure for
that. A very small cure, as she had no intention of going any

further with him than they'd already gone. But a little bit did feel right enough—enough to take away a little of the loneliness yet not enough to make her feel disloyal to Tom. Although admittedly she wasn't sure why being with Cameron even in the most casual of ways would make her feel disloyal like that. Crazy, mixed-up emotions, probably. "Getting involved hurts too much, Dag," she whispered. "I can't go through that again."

And even if she had the heart for it, why would any man want to get involved with her, anyway? After a hysterectomy, especially at her age—not even thirty—she wasn't exactly the answer to every man's prayers, was she? Somehow, a first date with a man, along with an explanation right at the start that she had no means by which to give him his future progeny, just didn't seem mutually compatible. That did hurt because she'd wanted children—even when she'd been a little girl, part of what she'd seen when she'd pictured herself all grown up was being a mother. But none of that for her now. "Which is just as well," she said on a sigh. "Saves me from having to get involved with anyone again, doesn't it? No babies in my life, no men who want a family either."

Dag rolled his eyes up to her, heaved a heavy sigh, then went back to sleep on the crocheted mat.

"You know, you're getting lazy," she said, sticking her foot out from under the quilt to give him a little nudge. To her ears her voice sounded so flat, so lifeless. Maybe it was she who was getting lazy, sitting here all day, all night, stuck in a dull routine that never changed, watching the world go by. "I think you need some exercise." She shoved off the quilt. "I think we both need some exercise." Something away from the front porch or the veranda out back or the parlor—the places where she spent most of her time.

Suddenly, the prospect of getting away didn't seem all that frightening. For the first time since she'd been here she actually did feel like taking a little walk. For a little exercise? Maybe some fresh air? Or, perhaps… No! She wasn't on the prowl for Cameron Enderlein, and she put that silly notion right out of her head. "I need exercise," she said aloud. "That's all it is!"

She thought about walking to town, which was only the distance of about three short blocks from her house, and perhaps while she was there she'd pick up a few groceries—make that her excuse to go, instead of having them delivered to her this week. Of course, that would entail meeting people along the way, and those people would ask questions and try to extend sympathy. She did appreciate the concern, but she didn't feel ready for it yet. Her adjustment was coming in stages—adjusting to her physical ills first, to her loss of Tom, to a life she wasn't sure she'd ever want back. Getting back into even the smallest social swing was still way down on her list of priorities and, truthfully, it frightened her. Made her feel exposed and vulnerable. So, while the walk to the grocery store was a simple thing, it was also a very complicated thing. But maybe she needed that now…needed something to shock her out of the numb routine she'd already set herself into here in Lexington.

"It'll get me out of my rut and, besides, you need some stimulation, too, don't you, boy?" she said to her dog. He needed it more than she did, actually. He was a good dog going to waste. As his owner, and especially as a veterinarian, she was concerned that he was suffering his existence in a new life much the same way she was—by going dull. As a vet, she always advised pet owners to exercise their dogs and keep them active, that the little things like that led to longer, happier, healthier pet lives. As a good veterinarian, she truly believed that for her animal patients, but yet she found that advice so hard to take for herself, and the same did apply. It was just so difficult to do now, however. "But we'll take that walk no matter how I feel about it," she said, keeping her fingers crossed that the people they would meet along the way wouldn't know her, or would feel too awkward to fuss very much.

Of course, she *could* go the opposite way, down the road to the river, perhaps meet Dr. Enderlein there if he'd managed to slip by her, unseen, this morning. Except, that really didn't suit any purpose. She was smart enough to know that she wouldn't recover fully, and get over all the emotions still pent up in her, if she didn't force herself into it, and avoiding going to town wasn't going to force anything.

"In other words, I'm the one who has to stop myself from wallowing."

Knowing what she had to do and doing it were two different things, though, weren't they? The rational mind acting against the spiritless ache that held her back and scared her to death over even the smallest step forward. "But I've got to do it, Dag. Don't I?" That's what her intellect was telling her anyway, while the rest of her was still fighting it.

She wanted someone to jump up and say *No, don't go,* but when Dag jumped up, it was with the expectant look that something exciting was about to happen for a change. The wagging tail was the give-away. "Then I guess that's it. We go to town." She said the words even though she didn't sound convinced.

Twenty minutes later, Dani looked at herself in the bedroom mirror, frowning. She was a mess. A complete, total mess. Her hair was scraggly and self-cut for so many months now because she didn't have the energy to go to a beauty salon. It looked like a frizzy mop on top of a pale face that was offset by sunken eyes surrounded by dark, puffy circles. The months of neglect had certainly taken their toll. Of course, that would have made a brilliant excuse not to go out, but Dani forged ahead, finding passable clothes—an ecru cable-knit sweater and black jersey slacks—both very bulky on her slender frame, concealing her weight loss. "Well, it's the best I can do," she said, wincing over how everything hung on her like a tent, practically dwarfing her to child-like proportions. Although somehow that made her feel secure, like people might not see her.

"Doesn't matter anyway," she tried to convince herself as she leashed Dag and headed down the front walk and through the rusty iron gate. But, honestly, she was bothered by what had stared back from her in the mirror. She hadn't noticed how awful she looked until just then, and it had been quite a shock. "So I've never been fashion conscious. And if someone wants to comment about the way I look…" Well, she wasn't sure what she'd do. Jut her chin and laugh at it? Cry? Apparently, time would tell, as she wasn't altogether sure about the state of her emotions. "Let's keep our fingers crossed, Dag, that I don't do something to embarrass you. *Or me.*"

Dani stopped and looked both ways up and down the road. It was hard to realize she hadn't ventured *anywhere* on her own since that day on the mountain, but she hadn't. Since then she'd been either confined or under tight medical supervision. Until she'd come here. So this moment had been an awfully long time coming, and the butterflies in her stomach testified to that. Absently, she bit her bottom lip as she patted Dag on the head, still toying with taking the road in the opposite direction of town where she was sure no one would bump into her. "Except that's not what you need, is it, boy?"

She glanced down the road toward town, saw it in the near distance, and immediately her hands began to shake. "And avoiding town's not what I need either. Just what I want." Her head seemed to be spinning a little, too.

Dag whined, and looked up at her, possibly sensing her confusion, possibly expressing his own. "OK, I'm not making any promises. We'll go as far as I'm able." The doctor had called it social anxiety—a fear of going places, meeting people. Not severe at this point. But serious enough to cause problems if she let it, and he had told her the more she kept to herself the more it would overtake her. "You've got to help me with this, Dag." Her voice wavered. "I need all the help I can get."

That seemed to suit the dog, because he tugged at the leash the way he used to when they had been on a rescue. Did he sense she was the one who needed rescuing here?

Reluctantly, Dani let him lead her in the direction she truly didn't want to go, and at a pace much faster than she was able to manage, even with so many months of physical therapy. "Slow," she ordered, and Dag immediately obeyed. They were halfway to town by now, and she could actually see people walking about on the main street.

Immediately, her heart started to pound, and her breath started coming in short gasps. Her head felt even lighter than before, like she might faint. "Damn it," she muttered, stopping. This was a simple walk, one she'd taken hundreds of times. It was a small town—one main road with several short offshoots. The businesses were cozy and home-owned. The people were friendly.

She knew these people! They cared about her. The cold sweat breaking out on her forehead, though, was a clear indication that she wasn't ready to deal with them.

For a moment, Dani considered turning around and trying to get back home before she passed out, and as she started to turn, she nearly bumped into Cameron Enderlein, who'd come up behind her. "Where did you come from?" she gasped, her head setting into a major spin.

"Originally, Boston," he said, smiling. "Just now from Mrs. Gardner's. I had a nice breakfast of blueberry pancakes in exchange for a little medical treatment."

"Shaving her bunions?" Dani asked, her breath now coming in little gulps. Tiny purple spots started floating before her eyes and her lips were beginning to tingle. "She…um…she always asks someone to do that for her. I've…um…I've been telling

her for years her proper shoe size is ten, not eight and a half…"
She wiped the sweat from her forehead then shut her eyes,
trying to catch her breath. "She's always going to…um…have
bunions until she…" Before she could finish the sentence, Dani
pitched forward, straight into Cameron's arms.

"Danica… Can you hear me, Danica?"

She could. But she wasn't ready to admit it. She was glad
to be back in her bed, all safe and secure.

Dani inhaled a deep breath, wondering where the lilac scent
of her sheets had gone. She always washed with lilac water…an
old-fashioned favorite of her grandmother's. And hers. These
sheets smelled…masculine, nice. She took in a deep whiff,
enjoying the pleasant, unexpected scent. Was it musk?

"Here, you need to drink this. Your blood sugar's low. I did
a finger stick and you're at fifty-two, which is probably why
you passed out. Your blood pressure is a little low, too, but everything else is fine."

Was Cameron Enderlein actually talking to her? Surely not.
He was making a diagnosis, though. Even in her bleariness, she
could hear that. Diagnosing hypotension and hypoglycemia.
No, that wasn't about her. Couldn't be.

"Danica, listen to me. I know you're tired. But either you
open your eyes and drink this or I'm going to have to start an
IV to get some glucose back into your system. Your choice."
He took hold of her hand and gave her a gentle slap on the wrist,
then rubbed her hand. "Danica, wake up."

My, he had a nice voice. She did like that about him. Nice
hands, too. Soft, gentle. That's all she liked, though, as he was
such a pushy man.

"Danica, wake up now. I know you can hear me. Wake up
and listen to me."

He gave her a little shake, and she felt it. Yes, Cameron

Enderlein was a very pushy man. She opened her eyes to tell him so, and saw right off she wasn't in her own bed. In fact, she had no idea where she was. It wasn't a hospital bed. More like a bedroom, but tiny, very plain. Not like her bedroom in her grandmother's house, all elaborate with a traditional Victorian flourish. "Where am I?" she asked.

"My room," he said, holding out a glass of sugary cola for her. "Now, drink it. I want to get your blood sugar back up."

It was all coming back to her now. Taking Dag for a walk, looking frowzy, feeling weak, her head spinning... "I fainted?"

Actually perched next to her on the side of the bed, not in a chair, not standing over her as a proper doctor would, Cameron nodded. "You fainted, but I caught you."

"And carried me to your...your bedroom?"

"Had a little help there," he admitted. "Couldn't manage both you and your dog. And it seemed more comfortable for you on my bed than an exam table. It was closer than my clinic, too, which is why I brought you here."

Dag! Immediately, Dani bolted up in bed, but a searing pain shot through her head, followed by a wave of nausea, and she crumpled back into the pillows. "Where is he?" she choked. "My dog?"

"Mr. Barnaby took him while I took you. He said he'll bring him up to your place once you're back there."

Paul Barnaby was the town pharmacist. He'd lived in Lexington only a couple of years, and she didn't know him well. The thought of Dag being with a stranger did concern her. "I'm fine," she said, trying to sit up again, "and I've got to go get my dog." By the time she was half off the pillow, Dani's head started to spin, and reluctantly she sunk back down again.

"You're two minutes away from an IV," Cameron warned, holding out the cola again. "So, how long has it been since you've eaten?"

"Last night," she said, taking the drink from him. Last night, maybe it had been lunch yesterday. Or breakfast. Days ran together and she didn't pay much attention to those kinds of things. Eating to sustain herself had been all she'd done these past months, and sometimes she simply forgot.

"Well, if that's true, you didn't eat enough to keep your blood sugar up. Have you had these attacks before? Because I'm wondering if we need to sit down and draw up a regular eating plan for you...meals, snacks, that kind of thing. Perhaps run some other blood tests?"

"No," she lied. "This is the first time." She wasn't about to let this man into her life as a doctor, or anything else. And a bit of hypoglycemia wasn't exactly anything to get in such an uproar over. Besides, she knew how to treat it! A little food, and she was cured. No assistance required.

"You're a little on the dehydrated side, too."

"So I forgot to take a drink of water this morning. Other than that, I'm fine, Doctor, and as soon as the sugar has time to work its way through my system, I'll be out of here." She took another drink of the cola and, amazingly, started to feel better. Hypoglycemia did reverse quickly.

"Two hours minimum," he said.

"For what?" she snapped.

"To stay here and rest."

"In your bed? You want me to stay *in your bed* for two more hours?" The bed with the nice-smelling sheets. Suddenly it occurred to her that they smelled just like Cameron.

"If the floor is more comfortable for you, that will be fine, too." He grinned down at her. "Or the chaise on the front porch. Your choice, Danica. But no matter what you choose, you're staying down for two hours. And if, in that time, your blood sugar and your blood pressure haven't elevated, I might keep you another two."

"Like you could," she snorted, trying to put up a good protest, but not feeling quite up to it yet.

"Actually, you don't look like you've got enough strength in you to fight me off."

"Are you always so rude, Doctor?"

"To my patients, no. But you're not my patient. Remember?"

"So you're admitting you're rude to your friends?"

"No, I'm not rude to my friends either. But you're not my friend. Your choice, not mine. Which means you're merely someone on the street who collapsed in my arms, then put up a squawk when I tried to help her. Drink more of that cola before Mrs. Gardner gets here."

"Why is *she* coming over?" The last thing she wanted was to have more people see her sprawled out in Cameron Enderlein's bed in this condition.

"She's bringing you blueberry pancakes and her home-made syrup. Lots of sugar in that, and I expect you could probably use a good meal."

Surprisingly, that did sound good to her. Not that she was hungry. But a few bites might hold her over until the next time she had to eat. "I'll go after I eat," she gave in, relaxing back into the bed and into the sheets with that wonderful scent.

"Then eat slowly, because I *still* don't want you up for a couple of hours." He reached out for her hand, and she recoiled, but he leaned over and took it anyway. Just as she was about to protest, she felt the slightest prick to her index finger. Then he gave it a good squeeze and dabbed a drop of her blood on the test strip. Thirty seconds later, he stood up. "Seventy-six," he said, walking over to the window and pulling back the curtains to let in the light. "Not great, but better. And I see your breakfast coming down the street now. So we'll do another finger stick in an hour, and if you're normal, I'll think about letting you go home a little early."

"In another hour, after you do the test, I'll let you know if I'm up to going home," she said, trying to sound in control, even though she knew she wasn't. Which was the problem. She hadn't been in control since that day on the mountain, and control over her life, more than anything else, was what she wanted desperately to get back.

She ate rather well for someone who protested about eating, Cameron thought. She'd gone through almost two of Mrs. Gardner's lovely pancakes before she'd finally quit, and now she was actually washing the dishes...ones left over from his late-night snack last night as well as the ones from her breakfast. Danica was an interesting woman. Cute, in a ragged sort of way. And so defiant...

Actually, he liked that about her. At some point he thought it would probably turn into independence because from everything he'd heard about her from practically everybody in town, Danica was nothing if not independent. Independent, bright, and a woman who knew what she was about, no mistaking that by anyone. That image of her did intrigue him, he admitted to himself. Not so much because he had any delusions about this. She was someone to watch over, that's all! And not watch over too closely, as in develop any kind of fascination. That wasn't his life now. Hadn't been for quite a while, and wouldn't be for quite a while to come. Living in the shadow of cancer, as he had been, didn't give you much else in your life other than the cancer.

Still, he did like watching her. More than that, he liked having a woman in his home, even if only for another few minutes. It filled things up, made it not quite so sterile. Amazing. He hadn't really missed that aspect of his life, having a real home again. Not at all. Oh, he'd had one in Boston. A nice townhouse about a block from his clinic. He'd entertained there, felt good there. Felt like his future had been there with

Sarah. He'd been wrong about all that, though. Every last aspect of it. Including Sarah. But to be fair, it hadn't been Sarah's fault. They'd both fallen victim to the circumstances. She'd hung on to the point where it had been destroying her, and he'd let her. She should have let go much earlier, or he should have pushed her away. But he'd allowed her to stay involved, and over the months had watched what had been good between them go bad in more ways than anyone would have guessed. Poor Sarah had been so valiant, when she should have been selfish. And he'd been so selfish when he should have been valiant.

So when he and Sarah had finally ended, and every last drop had been squeezed from what should have been a perfect relationship, he'd left everything behind to come here and figure out the next phase in his life. Now look at him. One little fainting incident, bring home one bedraggled woman, and here he was practically having fantasies of what it would be like to keep her here and make a real home of it.

Well, none of that. If nothing else, he was a practical man who was acutely aware of what he could and couldn't have right now. Yes, he was in remission from his leukemia, a good strong remission according to all the test results. But remission didn't mean cured, and he still had two years to go, cancer-free, before his oncologist would pronounce him cured. Then, *and only then,* would be when he would begin again. Everything else until that time was merely about waiting, and especially about *not* dragging someone else into that interminable wait. "Well, your blood sugar's one-thirteen now, which means you're normal, and good to go if you'd like."

Dani laid down the dishtowel and turned to face him. "I appreciate you taking care of me, Doctor—"

"Cameron," he interrupted.

"Doctor," she continued. "I should have recognized the symptoms but I thought it was nerves."

"A bit of agoraphobia?"

She blinked her surprise. "Does it show?"

"You're a recluse, Danica. I know you've had good cause to keep to yourself, but anyone who has a good case of nerves when walking down the main street of a town where everybody loves her has a problem. And I'm guessing yours is agoraphobia." That, and not eating properly. Which he wasn't going to address as she was a medical professional, another field but with nearly as much training as he'd had. So she knew how to deal with that, and he trusted she would. No need to nag her about it unless he saw other problems later on.

"I got counseling early on to help me cope, and my psychologist did mention that it was normal, under circumstances like mine." She returned the last dried plate to the cupboard and shut the door. "But I'm trying to go out more, and he said that if I keep forcing myself I'd get over it. It's not a severe case."

Not severe unless you combine it with hypoglycemia, Cameron wanted to say, but he was trying hard not to be too much of a doctor here. Danica needed a friend more than she needed a medic, and, for whatever reason, he wanted to be that friend. "And this started after your accident?"

"The doctor said so many months of being totally dependent was the cause. That, and the actual accident." She stared at him for a moment, like she wanted to say something, but after a moment of silence, she headed to the front door. "I appreciate you helping me, Doctor," she said. "Send me a bill for your services, and I'll phone Mrs. Gardner and thank her for the breakfast."

"No charge, Danica." He smiled. "I did it as a friend, and friends don't bill friends."

She looked rather surprised. "Again, I appreciate that." She opened the door, ready to step outside, then turned back around to face him. "Why are you here part time?"

"Cutting back in my life. It was getting out of control, and I got to the point where I needed to find something different. Not sure what it is yet, so I'm here, giving myself some time to think."

"My grandmother said you had a nice practice in Boston. Couldn't you have cut back there?"

"Couldn't you have recovered in Dallas? That's where your veterinary practice was, wasn't it? Your practice, your home, your friends. So why not hole yourself up there instead of coming to Indiana to do it?"

"Because people there wouldn't let me. They thought they knew better what I needed than I did."

"And people in Boston thought they knew better what I needed than I did. So I came here where no one has any expectations of me. Simple is that."

She gave him a thoughtful nod. "Nothing is ever that simple, Doctor. We both know that."

Yes, he did know that only too well. He'd survived cancer in Boston but had failed miserably there in the aftermath, which was anything but simple. "Perhaps we do, but wouldn't it be nice to think it could be simple?"

"Nice, but not practical. Look, on your walk tomorrow morning, if you pass by Nora's bakery and buy cinnamon buns, I'll be happy to make the tea," she said as she walked out.

"Well, I'll be damned," he said, half to himself. It wasn't the response he'd expected from her. It was better. And worse.

Trying hard to put Danica out of his mind, Cameron Enderlein grabbed up his medical bag, stepped outside, and watched Dani walk back to her end of town. Once she was out of sight, he went in the opposite direction to his office, keeping his mind full of medical signs and symptoms and assessment procedures, then resorting to listing all the various two hundred and six bones in the human body. Anything to keep himself from thinking of Danica, and her invitation to breakfast tomorrow.

* * *

Rather than heading straight home, Dani turned off Main Street onto Vine, walked half a block, then stopped outside Lena Harmon's shop and looked in the window. It was busy today, all three chairs occupied, and the manicure station taken up by Donna Jackson, who was actually getting a pedicure. She was tempted to go inside and ask Lena for a quick clip and a little restyling. Maybe even a few lighter blonde high-lights. The way she'd worn her hair previously. But there were so many people…

She looked in for another few seconds, then decided against it. But as she turned away, the salon door jingled open and Lena ran out onto the sidewalk, her arms wide open. "Dani!" she squealed, running up to her. "It's so good to see you!"

Without even a blink of hesitation, Lena grabbed Dani and gave her the hug only a huge, buxom woman could give. Lena, with champagne-dyed hair, bright blue eye make-up, rouge and massive gold jangling earrings and bracelets, spun Dani around, holding onto her. By the time Dani pulled herself away, Lena was crying, with great rivulets of muddy mascara running down her cheeks. "I wanted to call," Lena sniffled. "But I didn't know if you'd want that. People have said you were keeping to yourself right now, so I didn't bother you. I wanted to come see you, though, sweetie. Please, know I wasn't trying to ignore you."

"I know," Dani said uncomfortably. "Right now I prefer being alone. It's easier that way because people are awkward around me, don't know what to say…" Which was the truth almost as much as was she was just as awkward around people.

"I understand," Lena said, taking hold of Dani's hand. "After my Steven died I simply didn't want to see anybody for months. So I know exactly how you're feeling, which is why I've stayed away."

Except Steven had been her cat. But Dani didn't take

offense, because Lena meant well. "Do you have time to squeeze me in for a cut?" she asked tentatively.

"Do I have time for you? Of course I do, sweetie. And if you want, I'll tell everybody in the shop to go home and come back later, if that will make you feel better."

Actually, it would. But Dani wouldn't do that. Her problems were her problems, and she wasn't going to inconvenience anyone else with them. "I'll be fine," she said, as Lena dragged her into the tiny shop. Once there, staring into the faces of so many people she knew, she wasn't sure if she could go through with this. It was stifling, the walls closing in, and she could feel her hands starting to shake. "Maybe another time, when you're not so busy," she said, trying to pull away from Lena.

"Nonsense. You're here, and Lena's going to take good care of her little Dani." With that, Lena shooed Helen Gladstone from her chair and put her under the hairdryer, then rescheduled the other two women awaiting their appointments to come back in an hour, which they were happy to do when they saw it was for Dani. "So tell me," Lena said, running her fingers through Dani's hair, once they were practically alone in the salon, "do you want the old Dani back?"

Did she ever! In more ways than anyone could ever imagine.

CHAPTER THREE

IMAGINE that! Just a little brushing and her hair looked good again. Lena had worked a miracle with a quick cut and some highlights yesterday, and this morning the reflection staring back at Dani from the mirror nearly looked passable. Those make-up samples Lena had sent along home with her hadn't hurt any either.

"And, no, I'm not doing this on the slim chance he'll be stopping by with cinnamon buns," she said to Dag, who sat in the hallway, watching her primp. "I'm just trying to…to…" To what? Look better for absolutely no one? Look better for herself? Look better because she was hoping Cameron would stop by? She glanced down at her dog. "Doesn't matter what I'm trying to do. It feels good, getting fixed up a little. That's all, and that's enough." That much was true, too. It did feel good, and this was the first time since the accident she'd even cared about her appearance. Small steps, she thought as she took one last look in the mirror and smiled.

Downstairs, a few minutes later, Dani filled the tea kettle and sat it on the cold stove burner, just in case Cameron did stop by this morning, then went to the front porch and took her position in the white wicker chair, pulling her feet up under her as always and tossing the quilt over her lap.

Settled in, she twisted around in the chair restlessly, shifting and reshifting positions until, finally, she shoved the quilt aside. It made her look too much like an invalid, and enabled her to sit and watch the world go by rather than get up to participate. She'd counted on that feeling every morning for quite a while now as she'd tucked herself away under that quilt. But not this morning. Admittedly, she was a little self-conscious about it, and watching Cameron make his way up the slight incline in the road, carrying a white bag with him, as he was now, it suddenly seemed crucial that she didn't appear so frail to him.

"Morning!" he called cheerfully from outside the iron gate. Holding up the bag, he waved it, but didn't ask to be invited up. Was he waiting for an invitation? Trying to be respectful of her wishes?

"Good morning. Are those cinnamon buns?"

"Fresh from the oven. All ready to fatten you right up."

Fatten her up? How utterly unflattering, she thought dismally. Just when her spirits were lifted a blip above a flat line and she wasn't absolutely repulsed by what she'd seen in the mirror, here was a reminder of all the bad things that had happened to her these past months. Now she wished she hadn't invited him. Grabbing up the quilt that she'd just set aside, Dani dropped it over her lap and gave him a listless wave to come on up. "Kettle's on the stove," she said with absolutely no inflection whatsoever in her voice. "Help yourself if you want tea." She glanced at the bag of cinnamon buns, but her appetite for them was gone now, so she turned her head away.

"You're looking well this morning, Danica. I like the haircut."

She glanced up at him. "I look well enough, but too skinny. Isn't that what you're saying?"

He chuckled. "Just a figure of speech. And from where I'm standing, you look pretty good."

"Is that meant to flatter me, Doctor?" she snapped, only

mildly annoyed with Cameron, but hugely annoyed with herself for being so let down by what he thought. She shouldn't be, didn't want to be. But there it was anyway, and she wasn't happy about it. "Because it doesn't."

He dropped the bag on the table next to her. "What it's meant to do is let you know I've got hot cinnamon buns. Nothing else intended except casual conversation. So, do you want me to make the tea again? Or would you prefer I go away?"

"It's always so casual with you, isn't it?" Frowning, she twisted in her chair to get a better look at him. With the backlit light of morning coming over his shoulder, she saw the gold highlights in his hair. He *was* a handsome man. Maybe even breathtakingly so, had she been in the market. And she always felt a little twinge of attraction when she looked at him, followed by a huge dose of guilt. But she ignored the twinges these days. They simply didn't matter anymore. "You paste that smile on your face and pretend everything is fine and dandy, then expect everyone to respond to you the same way you give that casual attitude to them. Well, in case you haven't noticed, things aren't fine in my life, Doctor, and I'm just not in the mood to duplicate your cheerful attitude. Or deal with it. I appreciate the cinnamon buns, but you don't have to stay trying to analyze me, diagnose me, fatten me up or whatever it is you're tying to do. I'm fine here all by myself, just like I am."

"No, it's not always casual with me," he said, the friendly timbre in his voiced replaced with a solemn thread. "And I know things aren't fine. But I'm not trying to analyze, diagnose or treat you. Your grandmother asked me to watch you, and that's what I'm doing. As a friend, Danica. Only as a friend. *If you want one.*"

"I have plenty of friends, *thank you,* and I don't remember asking for another. Especially one who's here at my grandmother's request." She yanked the quilt up even further, then turned away from him.

"I'm not here, trying to be your friend, because of your grandmother. I walk by the house in the morning and wave to you because I promised her I would. I bring cinnamon buns and actually have the audacity to think we might be able to spend a few civil minutes together eating them and drinking tea because of *me*. I've heard nice things about you and I thought you might be worth getting to know. But I'm not going to force myself on you and I'm not going to put myself out simply to bang into your wall of resistance time after time. I really don't need the headache. I mean, I know what you've suffered, and I'm sorry for your losses, but I've been offering you my friendship and so far all you've done is slap it right back at me, which is pretty damned rude no matter what you've been through. So here's my last offer—my friendship. Take it or leave it!"

She didn't respond for another minute. Rather, she studied him. He was angry, his neck was red and she could see a little clench in his jaw. This was a new layer revealed in Cameron Enderlein, and it was nice. He wasn't all smooth and polished like he'd been trying to appear. There was a little grit to his texture, a few bumps in the unruffled facade. Her life had been so bland lately, just one lusterless day after another because that's the way she'd wanted it, but the good doctor had persisted enough to cut through all the flavorless shades, and in some strange way it felt good. Felt like she was finally emerging from her cocoon. "I like that," she finally said.

"What?"

"Your temper. It suits you. Somehow I thought my insults would roll right off you, but you can be provoked, and I like it."

He arched his eyebrows inquisitively. "And you think it's good that I can be provoked?"

"I think it's not so casual. I've seen too many conciliatory smiles lately, heard too many unsalted words. You just added some salt. And I like that."

"Meaning?"

"Meaning I'm sorry about my mood swings. Sometimes I hear myself saying things I wouldn't normally say, and it's a surprise they're coming from me. My doctor said it was natural during the recovery. That I'm still reacting more to the accident and not so much to what's going on around me."

"If that's an apology, I'll accept it."

"So…"

"So, what?"

"Your apology for blowing up at me?" She knew he wouldn't because, honestly, she didn't deserve one, but she was curious to see where he'd go with this. She was curious to see a little more of his texture.

He gave her an over-exaggerated, thoughtful smile. "Do you deserve it, Danica?" he asked in his stiffest voice, even though the twinkle in his eyes betrayed him.

"Maybe. But since I gave you an apology, I thought you might like the opportunity to make things equal between us." The lighthearted give and take between them was good. She and Tom hadn't really ever had banter like this. Usually they'd talked work, and medical procedures, and ideas for more efficient rescue techniques. No arguments. Not so much depth. All *very* casual. Or sexual.

"Well, it sounds to me like you owe me a thank you as, admittedly, you deserved it."

"A thank you?" She laughed at his audacity. "Only in your dreams, Doctor."

"If you're allowed into my dreams, does that make us friends?"

"Are you sure you want to deal with me?" she asked, suddenly serious. "Because I don't come with guarantees."

"None of us do," he said, also serious. "So how about for now we just call it two people who enjoy a good cinnamon bun together and leave it at that?" Cameron reached into his pocket and pulled out a small black case. "Here," he said, handing it over, then headed to the door into the house. "Have a look." That's all he said, then he was gone.

Dani turned the small black case over then unzipped it, to find a blood-sugar monitor, test strips, a lancet device and several lancets. She knew how to use it, of course. Even *her* patients had blood-sugar problems. As she looked at the device, she wanted to be offended by this, as he wasn't her doctor. But she couldn't get a good, indignant steam up because, as a medic herself, for both animals and humans, this was exactly what she would have prescribed. It was called being precautionary as she'd had one incident of low blood sugar in public, and Cameron was doing the sensible thing. So as much as she would have liked to have given it back to him and told him she didn't need it, she knew he was right about this. She did need to keep a better watch on herself. Especially as she did spend most of her time alone.

At least he hadn't insisted on doing the test himself. For that, she was grateful.

After a quick swab of her finger with one of the alcohol wipes inside, Dani did the finger stick, dabbed the droplet of blood on the test strip, inserted it in the monitor and waited ten seconds for the result. Seventy. That was enough to be called very low normal, but not high enough to be in the safe zone. She *was* going to have to watch herself.

Before Cameron came back, she tucked the black case into her pocket, but she left the torn foil wrapper of the swab out where he could see she'd used it. And she didn't say a word when he returned, carrying two cups of tea. She did notice him glance at the wrapper as he sat the teatray atop it, and give a brief, affirmative nod, but that was all. No mention, no questions, no interference. Perhaps he did respect her wishes a little after all.

"Do you like small-town life and small-town medicine so far?" she asked, tossing off her quilt as he sat down next to her.

"It's different. People have different expectations. They want their doctor to be personally involved, to be a friend…"

"And you can't do that?"

"I can, but it's not easy. I mean, yesterday, you knew why I'd seen Mrs. Gardner. You knew all about her bunions. In my former practice, with the exception of a very few patients, I didn't know those things off the top of my head, and I wasn't expected to. I ran an immediate care clinic, and my patients were in and out. Most of them I saw once, and that was it— they went back to their real physicians. It wasn't impersonal, but it was nowhere close to the personal relationship the people here expect from me. And to be honest, I don't mind knowing that Mrs. Gardner wears the wrong shoe size and is willing to suffer a bunion for vanity's sake, but I don't want to know that she saw Emelie Jansen sneaking over to Jeff Plimpton's house last night. Which is what they want me to know—that, or something like it."

"She did?" Dani gasped. "Emelie and Jeff again? I thought they were over with a year ago."

"And that's the point! Why should I have to know that they were over with a year ago?"

"Because that's what you get in a small town like Lexington, like it or not. For me, coming home to all the town gossip and chitchat is one of the things I've always loved doing. At least, until I became the center of it. But trust me, if you stay here long enough, you'll get used to it. You *are* going to stay, aren't you?"

"This veterinary practice of yours…you said it's in Texas?" he asked as he dumped six cinnamon buns from the bag onto a serving plate.

Talk about an obvious avoidance. He couldn't have been more obvious if he'd printed the words "None of Dani's Business" on a sign and stuck it out on the highway. Dani reached for a cinnamon bun and broke off a small bite of it.

"Dallas. Past tense. Sold it. Sold my condo, too." Then she popped it into her mouth. Pure ambrosia. It melted like butter, and her next bite was bigger.

"That's going to the extreme, isn't it? There, then here? Different worlds."

She shrugged as she swallowed. "I love Dallas. But I needed to come home. Home is where the heart is, and all that. My heart's always been here."

"Meaning you're not planning on going back there, even to live?"

"Meaning no plans, period. Not there, not here."

"So you were raised here?"

He really was working hard to head off all chat about himself. It was a little annoying, actually, because she did want to know more. "Not exactly. I'm from Chicago originally, but I spent a lot of time here with my grandmother. Holidays, school breaks, every chance I could. It always seemed more like home than anyplace else because I think I always had this ideal that home should be cozy and friendly. Chicago wasn't, even though my family was there…still are. But this…it was more natural to me." Time now to turn the tables. "So, tell me about you. Something other than the fact that you're not comfortable with your patients' bunions being town knowledge and that you gave up your Boston practice for this." She gave him a deceitfully innocent smile over her teacup. "Because the subject of *me* is getting pretty boring, don't you think?"

"Not much to tell. Like I said, it was time for a change, and this seemed good. And expedient, as there was already an opening for a doctor here."

A man of few words, apparently. Which was getting quite frustrating now. "Any family left behind?" Wives, ex-wives, future wives, children? She didn't ask, of course, but she wanted to.

"Lots of it. Three brothers, two sisters, parents, grandparents. All still in Boston, and all of them thinking I'm insane for coming here."

"Are you?" Another opening, if he cared to take it.

"Insane?" he asked, chuckling. "Probably. But time will tell, I suppose."

"For both of us," Dani said wistfully, as she popped the last bite of her cinnamon bun in her mouth, deciding not to pry further. She didn't want to push the limits of this fledgling, tenuous relationship beyond what it was because knowing more kicked them up to another level, and she certainly didn't want to be kicked anywhere. But, admittedly, she was curious about his life and even more curious about why he wouldn't talk about it.

"So, I suppose you heard the rumors about Nina Owens?" Cameron asked, as the previous conversation died out and there was a long, thick pause between them.

"I heard she stayed on as your office nurse after Doc Wilson retired."

"Well, the only news that's bigger than Edna's bunion is Nina's pregnancy. Five months along, now."

"She's pregnant?" She and Nina were almost the same age. They'd been best friends when she'd come to stay with her grandmother. Nina had married nearly five years ago and she'd been one of the bridesmaids. Nice traditional wedding, almost exactly like the one they'd planned together years ago as children. "I didn't know," she said, surprised she hadn't heard. She had talked to Nina briefly a few times since the accident, but there hadn't been a mention. Not one from her grandmother either. Probably an issue of sensitivity because that baby-bearing option had been taken away from her during one of her surgeries in Brazil. She was happy for Nina, but admittedly the news did sting a little because part of those girlhood plans she and Nina had made together had been about the children they would have and the names they would pick out. Typical little-girl fantasies. "People get a little touchy on the subject of pregnancy and babies around someone my age who's had a hysterectomy."

Did he know about that? she wondered, as she watched him for a reaction. His opinion of her condition really didn't matter, but she did want to see how he would respond. He didn't respond, though, not so much as a flinch. Not the surprised arch of an eyebrow, not even a tiniest of facial twitches. "You already knew that, didn't you?" she asked. "About my hysterectomy?"

"Small towns," he said, nodding. "And for what it's worth, I'm sorry."

She waited for the rest, that someday, when she found a man to love her, it wouldn't matter to him, that there were so many children to adopt, that life without having children could be fulfilling. She'd heard it all and now she was waiting for his addition. But none came. "That's it? You don't have some kind of wise advice or assurance to give me?"

"Losses happen in a lot of ways, Danica. We live through them, we survive, we thrive. It's called the triumph of the human spirit, and I admire that. Something I learned a long time ago is that it's not the losses in our life that count, but the way we handle them. I'm sure you've heard all the platitudes about losing the ability to have a child, so all I can say is I'm truly sorry. But in life things have a way of coming to us when the time is right, even though I'm not convinced that the timing is entirely under our control. When the time is right for you, though, if you want a child, you'll find a way to have one."

She blinked her eyes in surprise. Maybe, just maybe, she was growing to like this man more than a little bit. "Well, I'm happy for Nina. I know she's been trying to get pregnant for a while, getting discouraged since it was taking longer than she'd expected. Maybe I'll give her a call and let her know that I'm fine about my condition...and happy about hers."

He smiled. "I've put her on moderate rest to be safe, so she can't work for me any longer."

"She's OK, though, isn't she?"

Cameron nodded. "Fine. Just a precautionary thing. But I'm in need of some help now, and I was wondering if you would… I mean, just until I can find someone else."

She dropped her second cinnamon bun back onto the plate and stared at him. "Me? You've got to be joking? Right?" They'd gone from a nice moment to this. One instant she thought this friendship might work out, and now she was already reconsidering it. Working in a medical office right now? Cameron Enderlein, *of all people,* should have known she couldn't do something like that. Yet he'd gone and asked, which had ruined a nice morning between them.

"No. Actually, I thought it was a brilliant idea. I don't work full time, so physically it shouldn't be taxing on you. Besides being a veterinarian, you do have medical experience as a paramedic. So I thought you might like the opportunity to get out of the house and be active…do something worthwhile."

"Worthwhile? I did something *worthwhile* once, Doctor," she snapped. "It killed the man I loved, and injured me. I don't want anything worthwhile again. Which is why I'm here—so people won't expect anything of me other than what I'm doing right now." How dared he? Under the pretense of *friendship,* he'd come here only for the purpose of asking her to help him, to work in his office. He knew her circumstances better than most, yet he'd dared to impose himself in a way he didn't have a right to. They weren't friends, not now. She didn't owe him anything other than the cost of a blood-sugar monitor, which she would surely pay by check as soon as the mail carrier came by. Besides that…well, she was angry. In a small way, she even felt let down. Clearly, his intention with the cinnamon buns and friendship prattle had been to find himself an employee. Well, not today, not with her. "You're wasting your time here, Doctor," she said, standing to go inside. "I'm not a paramedic any more, and I'm not even sure I'll be returning to a veterinary practice any time soon. More than that, I'm not in the mood for morning tea and cinnamon buns any longer. *With you.*"

By the time Dani reached her door, she thought sure he'd have said something to defend himself or prove her wrong or, at least, be on his way. But as she pulled open the screen door and glanced sideways at him out of the corner of her eye, he was still sitting there, cinnamon bun in hand, making absolutely no attempt to move. "Did I make myself clear?" she asked.

"Oh, you made yourself perfectly clear. Your preference is to stay here all by yourself, every day, and shroud yourself in self-pity."

"Not self-pity." Her voice was tight, furious. "Healing. Not that you'd understand that."

Again, he didn't answer, which put Dani even more on the defensive. She didn't exactly have a fight with this man, yet she felt the need to defend herself against a slap that he'd never landed. Odd, the way he made her bristle over positively nothing. "I came here to be alone, to work out my problems in my own way, to get away from people like you who think you know what's best for me. Well, guess what, Doctor? You don't. You don't even have an idea of what I need, and I resent the fact that you'd come here, making a suggestion that I should do something *worthwhile.*"

Cameron took a sip of tea, then set the cup down on the side table. "Two weeks," he said. "Three weeks tops. That's all I want. Just someone to fill in until I can replace Nina, because she's not coming back. Her intention is to stay home with her baby…a little boy, by the way. And I do have an enquiry in at a medical registry for a replacement. I thought that since you have medical skills and nothing to do with your days…"

There he went again. Another assumption. "You *assume* I have nothing to do with my days."

He turned to face her, yet made no attempt to leave *her* chair, *her* porch, *her* life, which infuriated her all the more as he'd simply made himself at home there when she clearly didn't want him.

"Do you?" he asked. "I'm sorry. I didn't know that. If I had, I wouldn't have asked."

"What I do with my days is none of your business!" She finally stepped into the house and let the screen door swing shut after her. Rather than closing the white-paneled front door, however, she stood behind the screen, her arms folded tightly across her chest, her foot tapping an angry rhythm on the wooden threshold, watching and waiting for the insufferable Cameron Enderlein to leave her porch.

Five minutes later, after he'd finished his breakfast, he finally stood and started to walk away. But he paused at the screen door and stood so close to Dani, the two of them separated by mere inches and a screen, that she could smell his musky aftershave lotion. Very nice, she caught herself thinking again, immediately trying to switch her rambling thoughts to something else, like, how angry she was with him. With him standing so close, though...

"I know it's not easy, Danica." His voice was so uncharacteristically low it caused her to shiver. "When you accused me of not understanding, you were wrong. I do understand what you're going through. I understand *exactly* what it is. I know your need to be left alone. I know your ups and downs, your heartbreak, your mood swings, your feelings of isolation. *Your anger.* And I know why you hide underneath that quilt. Something else I know is that you have the ability to get past it. But only if you want to. A walk to town may seem like a big step to you, and in some respects it is, but if you don't follow it up with another big step, and another one after that, you're merely treading water and fooling yourself.

"I know I don't have any rights here, not to suggest anything, not to ask anything, not to demand anything, and I'm sorry my offer upset you. But it stands. It's another big step that's yours to take if you want it. If not…" He shrugged, then a gentle smile crossed his face. "Look, I'm fixing spaghetti tonight for my dinner. Seven o'clock. The dog is welcome. So are you. I live in the tan cottage next door to the Graysons, if you're interested."

After that, Dr. Cameron Enderlein sauntered off the porch, down the walk, through the rusty gate, and Dani didn't shut the front door until he was out of sight.

CHAPTER FOUR

"NO, I DON'T want to go!" she snapped into the telephone.

"Then why are you so grumpy?" Louise Fielding asked. Her voice was chipper as always, chipper but a bit winded this time. Playing tennis with the girls, she'd told Dani. The girls— every one of them over seventy. Dani had interrupted the last game in the match and it was quite evident Louise was in a hurry to get back. "Just tell him no and be done with him. He's not an idiot, Dani. He won't keep coming back if you don't want him to."

"But that's not it. I mean, why would he even suggest such a thing? You didn't put him up to it, did you?"

"Maybe he asked because he needs help and for some strange reason he thought you might be qualified—which you are, in case you've forgotten! And, yes, I asked him to look in on you from time to time. That's all. I take it he's done that."

Even her grandmother seemed to be turning against her. She hadn't expected that at all. "I don't need anyone looking in on me. I'm perfectly fine…"

"Well, if you're so fine, tell him not to come back. It's as simple as that. If you want to stay all cooped up there by yourself, then tell the man to go away, and he will. If that's what you *really* want."

"You sound just like him. He actually said I should be doing something *worthwhile*."

Her grandmother snorted over the phone. "Heaven forbid you should get involved in something worthwhile again!"

"I thought you'd be on my side."

"I *am* on your side, Dani. You know that. And if you need me there, you know I'm less than an hour away, and all you have to do is ask. But you do have to work this out on your own now. Your parents, your sister, me…we were all worried when you said you wanted to stay there alone in that house, but after I got over my own initial fear at having you there by yourself, I realized you were right about this. The rest of the journey is yours alone. No one else can do it for you…at least, that's what you kept telling us until we finally listened. So don't go second-guessing yourself, and don't go getting all upset over Cameron Enderlein. He'll leave you alone or he'll be your friend if you decide you want that. It's your choice, Dani, and, sweetie, it's nothing to get yourself so worked up over. People want to help, and because they care they'll say things that aren't necessarily what you want to hear. But at least they're trying."

"Are you implying that I'm not?"

"Only you know the answer to that. Now, I hate to cut you off, but I've got to go beat the skirt off Vivian Wentworth. Again!"

Her grandmother, the tennis queen. That brought a smile to Dani's face off and on for the rest of the day as she puttered about in the house, in the garden, back in the house, suddenly realizing she truly had absolutely nothing to do with herself. Funny how that hadn't mattered yesterday, and how it was driving her almost crazy today.

Cameron didn't expect her to come for dinner, not after what he'd said. Not really. It had been a sloppy invitation anyway, one he hadn't meant to extend. But it had popped out. No reason. Just a slip of the tongue. Danica didn't even want to leave her front porch, she hated him, and yet he'd gone and suggested an intimate little dinner for the two of them…and her dog. What the hell had he been thinking, doing something like that?

Problem was, he hadn't been thinking, or he wouldn't have done it. Inviting her begged interaction, begged trouble, neither of which he wanted.

But he wasn't too worried. She wouldn't show up after all the things he'd said. Most likely, she wouldn't even come outside in the mornings now until he'd passed her house on his walks. And what had he been thinking anyway, asking her to come and work in his office? Another sloppy invitation. Honestly, though, he'd thought it would be good for her. A little nudge in the right direction. She was so close to the edge of re-claiming her life, and he recognized that in her from a similar period in his own life.

For him the nudge had been Sarah. She hadn't meant to nudge him, but when he'd found out the depth of her personal anguish over not being able to deal better with his illness, es-pecially as she was a doctor, he'd known those had been con-flicts in her that would never resolve themselves until he had left. Hanging onto a desperate hope had been what he'd been doing. But she'd finally admitted her feelings, that she was struggling with the relationship, struggling to deal with his cancer, and struggling over the feelings that she had because people would believe her to be awful if she left him in the middle of his crisis. All that with the addition of the guilt she would feel if she left him—the guilt being her worst splinter of hell. Sarah's life had been falling apart, and that had been the nudge he'd needed to get him out of his old rut and start in a new direction.

He cringed, thinking back to Sarah's little nudge. Chemotherapy had been long over with, his hair growing back nicely, and she'd wanted to make love. They hadn't in over a year, and she'd been very good about it. She'd suggested that trying to spark the romance again would bring some normality back to their lives, but he hadn't been ready to have normality restored yet. It had been such a simple, reasonable thing for her to ask but he'd responded much the same way Danica had when he'd suggested she go to work for him. "So I was being stupid." A sentiment with which he heartily concurred but, still, he did want to help Danica in spite of knowing better than to push her.

Maybe it was the way she looked…so sad. Sometimes a spark of life flickered in her eyes, but mostly, in unguarded moments, all he saw was the deep, abiding sadness. She must have truly loved the man who had been killed to still be mourning him that way. Louise had told him most of the story, and people in town had filled in bits and pieces. Danica and…he thought the name was Tom hadn't been officially engaged, but apparently that had been a mere technicality, because everybody had known it was going to happen. In fact, Tom had come to Lexington with Danica on a short holiday before they'd been called to Brazil, and people still talked about them as such a good couple. The talk of the town.

But so much could happen to shatter a life in only the blink of an eye, as he well knew. "And it takes so much more than a blink to get it all back," he said aloud, as he stirred the spaghetti sauce he was cooking. Oddly enough, he was cooking enough for two. Enough for leftovers, he kept telling himself as he tossed a salad ample for two, cooked pasta enough for two, and placed two wineglasses on the table.

OK, so maybe some wishful thinking was involved here. Nothing romantic, though. Just friendly. That's all he allowed himself these days.

Cameron glanced up at the wall clock. Seven. So was he kidding himself? Off and on all day he'd played out the dinner

scenario, first one way, then another. One version had Danica
showing up, glad to be there. Or, at least, reasonably glad.
Another had her showing up, changing her mind once she was
there and leaving. And yet another had her not coming at all.

Truth was, he didn't know Danica well enough to predict her.
Given her ups and downs, even if he did know her, predicting
her wouldn't have been exactly easy, especially after making
such an idiot of himself that morning. He'd damn well insulted
her. Danica was fragile after all. He knew that, yet he had told
her to do something *worthwhile* with her life. Worthwhile! For
heaven's sake, the woman had almost got herself killed doing
something more worthwhile than anything he'd ever even
imagined, let alone done. "Do something worthwhile," he
muttered, glancing back at the clock. Two minutes past seven
now. "You're too damned out of practice, Cam. A little bump
in the road takes you out of the game, and you forget how to
play." And with Danica it wasn't even playing so much as it
was…well, he didn't know what it was exactly. Trying to be a
concerned friend? A brother of sorts? Was there a level of attraction he was trying to ignore? Whatever the case, one thing
was certain. His social skills needed some work. *Lots of work!*

Cameron glanced at the clock yet again. Another minute
passed, and it seemed more like ten. "She's not coming," he
said, pulling the pasta pot off the stove and draining the water.

After he'd dumped the pasta in a bowl, then dumped the
sauce into another bowl and carried them over to the table, he
looked at it. It was nicely set for two, and one candle shy of
being romantic, as only a single light shone over the entire
dining nook. Cozy, nice, all the right ingredients for a great little
date between friends, except there was no friend present. With
a sigh, he sat down and took one more look at the clock. Five
past seven now, and it was either eat, or let the food go cold.

"Oh, well…" he said, picking up the wine bottle to pour

himself a glass. Just as he tipped the bottle to the rim of his glass, someone knocked very lightly at his front door. At first, he wasn't sure he'd heard it, it was so faint. So he listened and, sure enough, a second knock followed the first.

Hurrying over, he opened the door, and stepped back. "I'm glad you could make it," he said, as Dag entered first, followed by Dani. "I wasn't sure that you would."

"I wasn't sure either, after everything that happened between us this morning."

"I was out of line, Danica, and I apologize for that. What I said about you doing something worthwhile..." Cringing, he shook his head. "I had no right."

"No, you didn't. But I'm not very easy to get along with these days, as my grandmother kindly pointed out a while ago."

He laughed. "I'm sure she did it in a way only a grandmother can get away with."

"I'm sorry for overreacting," Dani said. "Sometimes I think I look for reasons to overreact. Something to lash out at, to be angry with."

"And I'm sorry for giving you something to overreact about. You've lived a very worthwhile life and I think I was just trying to shock you back into it. Which was wrong." He escorted her in, and the figurative distance between them was stiff and awkward. This was very difficult, and he really didn't want it to be. "So, I know this isn't the most gracious way of doing it. You're supposed to offer drinks and hors d'oeuvres, and give people a chance to relax before you serve them the meal. But dinner's on the table and it's getting cold." Thank heaven for that, because somehow he doubted drinks and hors d'oeuvres would relax anything between them.

"You weren't waiting for me?"

"Would *you* have waited for me?"

Dani pulled off her jacket, tossed it over the back of one of the two chairs in the living room, and headed for the dining nook. "Absolutely not, especially when something smells this wonderful." She smiled, tightly at first, then she relaxed into it. "Thank you for inviting me, Cameron."

Sauce from a jar, pasta from a box, salad from a bag, frozen bread... Maybe it wasn't the best of culinary efforts, but suddenly it seemed like a veritable feast. All because of his dinner companion.

"That was delicious," Dani said, carrying her plate to the sink. Overall, dinner had been pleasant. The conversation had been light, most of it inconsequential, which was fine with her. But her host had been charming. In fact, he'd been so charming she hadn't even noticed how much she'd eaten until there had been nothing left on her plate. He'd served her up a rather large portion, about as much as she would normally eat in three days, and she'd done all but lick her plate clean.

"If I can open the jar or the box, I'm a great chef. Other than that, I make sandwiches or go out to eat."

"You go out here, in Lexington?" She laughed, thinking about all the choices. Two of them. Both diners. One opened early and closed early, the other opened late and closed late.

"Well, let's just say that on occasion I get tired of sandwiches. I'm not much into domestic skills."

"Your house is tidy," she commented, setting her dishes aside.

"Came furnished. Landlady comes in twice a week to clean."

"Mrs. Milford?"

He nodded. "None other than."

"And she tries to fix you up with her niece?" She tried to fix up every eligible male between the ages of twenty and death with poor Amanda. Problem was, Amanda wasn't marriage material. She didn't particularly like men. Of course, she wasn't overly fond of women either. Mostly, she preferred cats. Lots and lots of cats. But for her aunt, hope always sprang eternal.

"Every time she comes to clean. Then a few times in between."

"That means you're a real part of the town, then. She only goes after the good, solid citizens."

Cameron carried his plate over to the sink, folded his arms and leaned against the counter. "What I am is the object of every mother's wish for her daughter. If I accepted all the dinner invitations I receive, I couldn't fit through the door."

"Not particularly fond of dating the locals, are you?"

"Not particularly fond of dating."

That said with a bit of an edge, she noticed. Edge, or regret? "Well, that's just as well as there's really no place to take a date around here." Was he burned out? she wondered. Broken heart, maybe? He could have been involved in a horrible divorce. Or… She took a glance at him while he gathered up the rest of the dishes. Nah. He definitely wasn't gay.

So what made Cameron Enderlein bitter? Or a man of deep sorrows?

She was fighting the urge again to ask him, but she wouldn't. He wouldn't answer even if she did, so it was best to leave this as a casual date. And, really, it wasn't even a date, casual or otherwise. It was merely two people eating together, indulging in very guarded, safe conversation. "Can I do the dishes?" she asked, as he brought the rest of them over to the sink.

"You're the guest, and the guest doesn't work."

Meaning, end of evening, and he didn't even have to throw that out as a hint. She knew it was time. "Then I think I should be getting home."

"So soon?" he asked.

"It's been months since I've done…well, practically anything. I'm feeling a little tired." Awkward excuse, but not a lie. She was tired. And to be honest, she didn't want to spend the rest of the evening talking about Edna's bunions, Amanda's cats or herself, which was what would happen. So it truly was time to go home.

"Then I'll drive you. Just let me grab my car keys."

"I'll walk, thanks. The night air will do me some good and it's only a few blocks. And Dag needs his exercise."

At the mention of his name, Dag bolted up and headed for the door.

"Then I'll walk along with you."

"You don't have to," she said. "Lexington is one of the safest towns around here." Even though she'd refused, she secretly hoped he would walk with her anyway. Somehow, a nice moonlight stroll with a dog seemed rather pathetic, but with a handsome man…

"You're not going to rob me of the chance to walk off that gastronomic masterpiece I created, are you?" He patted his absolutely flat belly. "Got to keep fit for my patients."

"And for Amanda Milford," Dani teased on her way out the door, very tempted to pat his belly, too. Of course, she didn't. But she knew it would not only be flat, but hard, and a smile crept to her lips, thinking about it.

They'd barely made it to the street when Greg LeMasters, the town sheriff, squealed the tires of his police car as he turned the corner and came to a dead stop right in front of Cameron's house. Greg was Dani's age, and she'd known him most of her life. Nice man, nice wife, nice kids. Life had gotten Greg everything he'd wanted. "Got a bad one up on the highway, Doc. Need some medical help up there right now."

Cameron gave Dani an apologetic smile. "Duty calls," he said, as the sheriff opened the car door for him. "Sorry about the walk."

"I understand," Dani replied. "And thanks for dinner. With everything I ate, I really do think you fattened me up a little." Smiling, she was about turn away and head home when all of a sudden Dag bolted, jerking the leash from her hand and lunging straight through the open door of the police car. "Dag," she shouted, "Come."

The dog refused.

"Come!" she said again, trying to sound even more firm about it. But Dag wasn't about to budge, and even Cameron couldn't shove him out the door.

"Look, Dani," Greg said, not bothering to hide his exasperation, "I've got to get going. Get the dog out, or he's going to come with me. Or you get in with him and ride along, and I'll have someone take you home later."

"Dag," she commanded frantically one more time, but to no avail. Dag's intentions were clear. He was going to a rescue. He sensed it.

"Dani!" Greg shouted. "Right now!"

There was no choice. Greg had to go, and she wasn't about to allow Dag to go without her in the hope that someone would watch out for him. So Dani jumped into the back seat next to her dog, who was sitting next to Cameron, and off they went to something she already knew she wasn't ready to face.

The ride was blessedly short, and throughout it, nothing raced through Dani's mind—no words, no thoughts, not even any fears. She was a total blank for those drawn-out moments, without even unconsciously counting the beats of her racing pulse or the shallow breaths she was exhaling with expediency. Nothing at all registered except the fact that nothing was registering, and by the time they'd reached the scene of the accident, her hands ached from balling them so hard into fists.

As the patrol car came to a stop, she immediately grabbed for the doorhandle, only to find there wasn't one. Then she remembered that was routine. No access to get out from the back seat of a police car, which was a terrible thing to thump her back into thinking because, immediately, a panic reaction set in. Claustrophobia. Couldn't get out! Couldn't breathe! She started to choke, gasping for air, just as Greg LeMasters opened the door on Cameron's side.

"Just sit here," Cameron said. "Breathe slowly, and you'll be fine."

"Fine," she murmured, fighting to regain her composure. "Easy for you to say."

"I can't stay here with you, Danica. You're having a panic attack, doing some hyperventilating, but you already know that. And I can't nurse you through it."

"I'll be fine," she snapped, not angry at him but embarrassed by herself. This shouldn't be happening. She should have better control. "Just go. I can take care of myself."

Cameron regarded her for a moment, gave her hand an affectionate squeeze, then climbed out and bent back down to look in at her. "I enjoyed our evening, Danica. Sorry it had to end this way." After that he was off, and she was alone, except for Dag, who was whining to get out on the rescue.

"No, boy. Not any more. That's not our life now." Which meant absolutely nothing to Dag, because even before she was finished saying the words, he bolted out the back door, determined to do the thing he most loved to do. Go find someone to rescue.

"Dag!" she shouted, but to no avail. He was already gone off on the job. Alone! And she couldn't allow that. She had to get him back.

Bracing herself for what she might see outside, Dani climbed out of the car, and immediately her head started to spin. Then her stomach turned over so hard she barely made it to a clump of weeds at the edge of the road, where she dropped to her knees and surrendered every bit of the dinner she'd had with Cameron. Once she'd retched herself into dry heaves, she stood back up, embarrassed for the display, and saw that everybody there was busy doing something important, and nobody had even noticed her. Except Cameron, who, illuminated by the headlights of one of the police cars, was bending over a patient but looking straight at her. "So what's one more humiliating display," she muttered, turning her attention to finding Dag, "other than a guarantee he won't be bringing me cinnamon buns any time in the near future?"

Even though he was a doctor, it was embarrassing. For a reason she couldn't define, she wanted to look...*stronger* for him. Well, that little fantasy had just come to an end, hadn't it?

Turning so she didn't have to see Cameron, Dani listened for Dag. She could hear him barking off in the distance. Unfortunately, that distance turned out to be right at the heart of the accident scene and there was such confusion going on all around her she couldn't get her bearings on what direction his barks came from. Which didn't matter at the moment because she was standing in the middle of a four-car accident, with the two that she could see in front of her badly mangled. Two weren't quite so bad, she thought as she started to assess the situation like she would have done before. Take a look, make an assessment, get to work.

Except she didn't do that now, and she had to remind herself that was the case. Cameron was here. There were others to help. All she needed to do was find Dag and walk home...distance herself from all this. Leave it to those who wanted to do it. Not to someone like her, who didn't.

Still, there was that twinge that told her she couldn't just walk away. The one that kept her looking and making mental assessments on what needed to be done. "No," she whispered, shutting her eyes to concentrate on Dag. "I can't."

She couldn't. Wouldn't. And she felt so...guilty. It was like she was there, up close and personal, but so far away. Everything was acute and vivid, yet somehow in a blur. She was the casual observer sitting in the audience, looking at a horror story playing out on a flat movie screen. But she was being pulled hard to do more than observe because people were yelling, people were crying. They needed help. They needed…her. And somewhere in the distance, Dag was still barking the bark that told her he'd found a survivor.

"Ma'am?" someone cried, grabbing hold of her arm. "Can you help us?"

She immediately shook her head and pulled away from the woman.

"Please, my husband. My son…"

"I'm not…" she started to say, then in the dim light from the headlights of the few vehicles that surrounded the accident site she saw that the woman had a horrible facial contusion of some sort. Immediately, she stepped forward and gently tilted to woman's head back into better light for a closer look. Forehead gash, not serious in and of itself, but it was a bleeder. And she could have a concussion or some sort of skull fracture. Without a penlight she couldn't assess pupilary reaction, so she did the next best thing. She held up her index finger in front of the woman's face. "Follow my finger," she instructed, then watched the way the woman's eyes followed right, then left. A little sluggish, but essentially normal. "I need to have you sit down," Dani instructed. "You have a head injury and out here it's too difficult to see what it is. So what I need for you to do is sit down, and don't get up until we're ready to take you to the hospital. Will you do that for me?"

"But my husband and son…"

"Where are they?" Dani asked.

"Over there. That car on the end. They're both hurt…"

The woman's words were getting a little slurred, but Dani didn't see any changes, and guessed fear, pain and exhaustion were the causes. "I'll take care of your family, but you need to take care of yourself. Do you understand?"

The woman nodded, and Dani helped her sit down on the curb at the side of the road. "I'll be back in a second." Without another thought, she ran over to the closest of the half-dozen police cars now on the scene. "I need a blanket," she shouted. "Right now!"

"Sure thing, Dani," Kyle Barlow, another old friend, said, grabbing one from the trunk of his car. He tossed it to Dani who ran back to the woman and wrapped it over her shoulders. "Now, tell me about your husband and son."

"They got out," the woman began breathlessly. "My husband's fine, but my son…trouble breathing. He collapsed."

Dani was instantly alerted. "Does he have asthma or any other kind of condition or illness that causes breathing problems?" Immediately, a dozen different examples clicked through Dani's brain.

"No. Nothing."

"Any other medical problems or recent injuries?"

The woman shook her head. "He was in the front seat with my husband. The seat belt caught him across the chest."

So many scenarios with that, and most of them not good. Seat-belt injuries could be horrible sometimes—broken ribs, punctured lung, tension pneumothorax. "I'll take care of him," she called back as she ran to find Cameron. Or, more suitably, Cameron's medical bag, since every procedure she might be required to perform needed medical equipment.

"Need oxygen," she said, dropping to her knees next to Cameron as he stabilized the leg fracture of one of the victims. "Needle, chest tube…"

"What do you have?" he asked.

"Don't know yet. Haven't had a look, but I'm guessing, from what his mother described, it could be a tension pneumo." She rummaged through his bag and found a large barrel syringe with a big-bore needle, along with Cameron's blood-pressure cuff and stethoscope, but that was all. "Can I take these?" she asked.

"Take anything you need. And we do have paramedics *en route* now so you'll have your oxygen and chest tube shortly." He laid a gentle hand on Dani's arm as she stood back up. "Are you up to this? You can finish here for me and I can…"

Cameron's voice was so filled with concern she felt the gooseflesh rise on her arms. "I have to be up for it." Being involved in an emergency rescue wasn't anything she ever wanted to do again, but here she was, doing what was second nature to her, and there wasn't another choice. She had to do it. Nothing in her, including the drop-dead fear she was feeling, could make her walk away from someone in need of help. "I'm fine," she said. "I appreciate your concern, but you don't have to worry about me. I can do this."

"I know you can do it, but I do worry about you, Danica," he said seriously. "More than you know."

He meant that, and it stunned her. "Thank you," she whispered, pausing a moment to give his arm a squeeze. In that passing second their eyes locked and she felt warmth flow all the way through her. "Cameron, I…" Her breath caught in her throat and her pulse quickened, but not from a panic reaction. "I've got to go." She broke the connection between them and ran to the last car in the procession of crashes and there, on the ground, found the father and his son, father holding onto son and son struggling to breathe.

"It's getting worse," the man cried. "He seemed fine when we got out of the car, but then he collapsed, and his breathing has been getting harder ever since."

Dani nodded, dropping to her knees. Her first action was to rip open the boy's shirt and observe his chest. Asymetrical chest expansion, meaning both sides weren't rising the same. She took a quick listen through the stethoscope, confirming her suspicion immediately. The right side, which wasn't expanding to its fullest, had substantially decreased breath sounds. Something was preventing the air from getting in. "His name?" she asked.

"Jeremy. Jeremy Lawson. I'm Anthony."

"Jeremy," Dani said, bending lower to the boy. "I know you're having a tough time breathing right now, but I'm going to take care of that in just a minute. My name's Dani, and I'm a…" She paused. These were words she never expected to say again. "I'm a paramedic. And what I need for you to do right now is relax. I know that seems tough, but do your best. Do you understand me?"

The boy, whose eyes were wide with fright, looked Dani straight in the eye and nodded. What she saw there was trust. Complete, unquestioning trust. Suddenly, her hands began to shake and she felt her own breaths trying to constrict in her chest. *Not now!* This boy expected her to save his life. She couldn't panic. *Not now!*

"Will he be all right?" the father asked.

"I'm doing everything I can to help him. What I need you to do is run back to the front of the accident and wait for the ambulance. I need oxygen here as fast as I can get it. Can you do that for me? Signal them over here as soon as they arrive." One thing she'd learned from long experience was that involving bystanders, especially family or friends, in the rescue was often a good way to keep them distracted. In Jeremy's case, his father didn't need to be here to see his son suffer.

Without a moment of hesitation Anthony Lawson jumped up and ran a straight past the collided cars to the area where the ambulances would park. While he did that, Dani took the boy's blood pressure—too low. And measured his heart rate—too fast. In addition, as she probed his neck area, she discovered that his trachea had shifted a bit and his jugular vein was distended. His respirations were three times the normal rate, leaving Jeremy panting like a dog, trying to get air in.

Dani was sure of the diagnosis. There was no doubt it was a tension pneumothorax. He'd taken a good pop to the rib cage with the seat belt, probably broken a rib that had poked through his lung. Now the lung was collapsing and air was filling the space it normally occupied. She had to get that air out, and keep it out in order to allow his lung to re-expand into that space, and heal. A simple procedure would start the recovery and Jeremy would feel almost immediate relief. "I'm going to stick a very large needle into your chest. It may hurt a bit, but you'll be able to breathe easier," she said, as she removed the syringe cap and prepared for the needle decompression.

"Danica!" Cameron called, running up to her. He had a package with a chest tube, and behind him Anthony was leading two paramedics who were bringing oxygen. "Let me do that!" Cameron said, kneeling down alongside her.

"I'll do the needle, you do the chest tubes," she said, her voice much more calm than she felt. Although admittedly she did feel better now that Cameron was here.

Taking a quick antiseptic swab of the area, Dani inserted the needle, and immediately felt that little pop into the chest cavity, then smiled as the air trapped inside in the wrong place literally rushed out the syringe. She drew in a deep breath as Jeremy finally did the same, then moved aside to let Cameron and the paramedics finish the procedure.

"Good work," he said, as he proceeded to do the minor field surgery that would allow Jeremy to keep breathing.

Yes, it was, she thought. But now that it was over, at a time when she usually felt exhilarated, all she could feel was numb. Numb, tired, sick to her stomach again. And all she wanted to do was find Dag, go home, shut the doors, pull down the window blinds, crawl under her quilt and never come out again.

As Cameron was about to slip the chest tube into Jeremy, Dani stood and walked back to the spot where she'd last heard Dag. "Dag," she called, then listened. Sure enough, he responded. The same bark she'd heard earlier. He was telling her he had a live victim.

"Is everybody accounted for here?" she asked Greg LeMasters, who was busy flagging in the first tow-truck that would, shortly, start removing the pile of crushed vehicles.

"Yes. Nine victims altogether. Two criticals, including the one you and Doc took care of, six not so bad, and, unfortunately, one fatality. The one who caused it. She swerved over the line…" He gestured Dani back as he flagged the tow truck in closer. "No smell of alcohol, so we think she may have dozed off or been distracted. I suppose the tests will tell us more."

Dani stepped away, and again heard Dag off somewhere, trying to tell her something. This time she decided to trust her instincts, treat this as a rescue, and go see what, or who, he'd found.

The underbrush and weeds along this stretch of road were particularly patchy, and it took Dani several minutes to get through to where she could hear Dag's barking better. He knew she was coming now, and the closer she got, the more frantic his yipping turned. "I'm on my way, boy," she cried, picking up her pace. This wasn't a false alarm. Dag didn't have false alarms, and to prove that, a little tingle was shooting up the back of her neck. Adrenalin pumping, nerves acute… All signs she knew well, that caused Dani to quicken her pace even more until she reached her dog. Then she stood there, frozen for a moment, before she dropped to her knees next to the child over whom he was huddling.

The first thing she did was assess the boy's pulse. A little rapid, but steady. His breathing was steady. But he wasn't conscious. He was warm enough, though. No hypothermia, so he hadn't been out here long. Had he been thrown from one of the cars in the accident?

She scooped him up, gave Dag the order to come, and ran back to the area of the crash. "Cameron," she screamed. "I've found another victim. Boy, probably three years old." Greg LeMasters had said everybody was accounted for, so how could someone have forgotten their child?

"On my way," Cameron shouted from somewhere down the line.

"Mama," the little boy cried softly.

"No, sweetheart, I'm not your mama. But I'm going to take care of you until your mama comes to get you."

"Mama," he whimpered again, snuggling into her chest.

Instinctively, she held him tight, then sat down on the ground and waited for Cameron to come. And rocked the child while she waited, wondering what kind of mother would have forgotten something so precious as this little one. Certainly, had she ever had the good fortune to have a child of her own she wouldn't have forgotten. No matter what, she wouldn't have forgotten.

"Robby Tilton," Cameron gasped, then he shut his eyes. "His mother…she's the one…"

"Oh, my God," Dani gasped, handing the child over to Cameron.

"No sign of anything serious," Cameron called out from the back of the ambulance. Danica was sitting on the ground outside and he was concerned about her. She hadn't said a word in the past twenty minutes. She'd just sat there, huddled under the blanket one of the paramedics had given her, and stared up at the sky. Dag was at her side, resting his head on Dani's lap.

He knew this would be too much for her. Too many bad memories. She been thrown into a situation and forced to respond, but she wasn't ready for it. And now, emotionally, she was isolating herself just like she tried to do up there on the hill in that big old rambling Victorian house of her grandmother's. It concerned him. To all appearances, she was healing well physically, but it was the emotional healing that was still so fragile for her, and at the point where she'd finally begun to climb out of her shell—this!

As a doctor, it wasn't any of his business since he wasn't *her* doctor. As a friend, though, he was worried. "I'm going to send him to the hospital for observation and have them watch him until we find someone to take him."

Dani nodded, but didn't speak, and Cameron had the overwhelming urge to sit down on the ground with her and pull her into his arms to reassure her that everything would be fine, the way she'd done with the little boy. The child had wanted Danica's comfort, though, while he was afraid Danica wouldn't want anybody's. And because she was so frail, he wouldn't offer. Not yet.

"I'm going to ride along with him," Cameron continued. "Make sure he gets settled in, order a couple of tests and some X-rays. I'll let you know how he's doing as soon as I know something myself."

Again, she merely nodded. Then, as the paramedic shut the ambulance door and ran around to climb in behind the wheel, Cameron stared out the back window at Danica, a feeling of helplessness washing over him like he'd never felt before. Sitting there alone on the cold ground, wrapped in a thin blanket, she was a sight that broke his heart because he knew what she was feeling. He knew that kind of pain, knew how deep it went, how badly it hurt. Most of all, he knew the sense of utter loneliness that went with it, and the feeling that nobody else in the world could understand it.

He understood it, though. All of it.

As the ambulance pulled away, for the first time in his life he was torn over doing his medical duty. He had to stay with the child. He was ethically and morally bound. But if that ambulance suddenly stopped, he knew he would jump out the back door and return to Danica. Everything else be damned.

The ambulance didn't stop, though, and once they were off the crash site and back on the main highway, Cameron finally sat down and took hold of the little boy's hand. "She saved your life," he whispered, feeling for the child's pulse. In spite of everything she had to have felt throughout the ordeal, all the raw emotions returning, the panic attack that gripped her now, Danica had done what she'd had to do. She'd found a way to do the thing she most feared, and he admired that. "You're one lucky little boy."

And he was one lucky man, getting to know someone like Danica. One lucky man getting to know a woman who didn't want anyone bothering her. Yet he wanted to bother. He'd promised himself he wouldn't, told himself he couldn't, but right now all he wanted was something he had no right to even think about.

Sighing, Cameron tried to put Danica out of his mind as the ambulance siren screamed through the night. As hard as he tried, though, he couldn't.

CHAPTER FIVE

THREE in the morning. She'd been pacing ever since Greg LeMasters had dropped her off five hours ago. Too nervous to sit, so she paced. Too keyed up to sleep, so she paced. Back and forth, out to the front porch then back inside the house. Up the stairs then down. Dag had been pacing with her through most of it, not sure what to make of her actions. He was at the ready for another rescue, but there would be no more. *Not ever again.*

What if she hadn't been able to treat Jeremy's tension pneumothorax, or even diagnose it? He could have died right there. Just thinking that caused the shaking in her hands to start all over again. Sure, there was the bright side. If Dag hadn't been there that toddler might have gone unnoticed and died of exposure out there in the cold all night. Or he could have wandered out onto the highway, or across the field into the stream. There were so many bad things that could have happened, yet she couldn't think of how she'd just saved him. Not when the thoughts of failing Jeremy kept beating away everything else, even though she hadn't failed him.

"Worst-case scenario," she said to Dag, as she fixed herself yet another cup of hot tea, hoping the warming effect would help her doze off. "I know it didn't turn out that way, but it could have. I had no business being out there." No business because she was jittery, because all her self-confidence had been left behind in the mud on that mountain where Tom had died. Dead and buried together—Tom and everything she used to be.

Dani glanced at the clock on the kitchen wall. It had ticked off only two minutes since the last time. She wanted morning now. She wanted to see the sun. It was still four hours away, but maybe when she saw it she would finally be able to sleep.

As she poured a little more hot water into her teacup and started to dip the bag back in, a knock at the front door startled her so badly she dropped the teabag on the floor and all but dropped the teacup. People around here weren't out this late, and they certainly didn't knock on other people's doors, so Dani was instantly alarmed. Quick steps took her straight to the phone on the wall at the back door, and as she picked it up to dial, another knock, this one louder than the first, ripped all the way through the house. "Danica!" a voice yelled. "It's Cameron. Let me in."

Her first thought was about Robby, and instant panic rose in the form of nausea. Had something gone wrong? Had he been more seriously injured than she'd thought?

"Danica, please, let me in."

Fearing the worst, Dani walked slowly to the front door, then peeked through the lace curtains to make sure it was Cameron, even though she had recognized his voice. When she saw him, she opened the door to the length of the security chain, her mind still clicking through all the things that could have gone wrong in the past hours—undetected head injury, internal damage… "Tell me," she gasped, fumbling to unfasten the safety chain. "What's wrong?"

"Everything's fine," he assured her. "Both boys are resting comfortably for the night."

"Thank God," she whispered, leaning against the doorframe to allow the anxious moment to pass. "I was afraid…"

He took hold of her arm, steadying her on the way to the love seat in the parlor, where he sat down and pulled her along with him. "You haven't slept, have you? You're exhausted, Danica, and I'm not saying this as a doctor but as a friend. You look like you're about ready to collapse and you know better, yet look what you're doing to yourself—not eating, not sleeping. All this worry doesn't help. You've got to get some rest before you end up back in the hospital."

She sighed heavily. "I'll sleep when I need to." When she could. When it wasn't dark outside. When her mind didn't twist with so many sad thoughts.

"You need to do it right now," he said gently.

It did sound good and, for a moment, she actually thought about resting her head on Cameron's shoulder and trying to doze off. He was safe, and safe was what she needed to help her sleep. Not tea, not drugs. But as quickly as that notion came, she shook it off. She wasn't entitled. Not to Cameron. Not to anyone. "Tell me about Robby," she said. "Did they find someone from his family to take him?"

"Not quite the happiest ending there, I'm afraid."

Dani sucked in a sharp breath for this, then held it.

"Unfortunately, we weren't able to locate anybody to take him for the night. I went back to my office and looked through the files and couldn't find any next of kin. Linda, his mother, was the only one listed, except for her mother, who's in a home for people with Alzheimer's."

"His father?"

Cameron shifted positions. "I don't suppose it's violating medical confidentiality now that Linda is dead, but she was inseminated. She'd hit forty, no prospects of marriage, mother in a deteriorating condition, and she desperately wanted a child."

"Brave woman," Dani said. "I can understand how she felt."

"Very brave. She was devoted to Robby."

"You knew her well?"

"As a patient, well enough. I've seen them both on several occasions."

"I'm sorry," Dani said. "It's not easy, losing a patient."

"I'm sorry, too. For Linda, for not getting to see her son grow up. And especially for Robby, for losing someone who positively adored him. Robby was her entire life."

"So what will happen to him if they don't find a family member to take him in?"

"I hope they will," Cameron said, but his voice didn't exude its normal confidence with that pronouncement.

Now that it was over, now that she knew everybody was safe, Dani was suddenly sleepy. So sleepy, in fact, she wasn't sure she could drag herself all the way upstairs to bed. "Thank you for coming to tell me. I appreciate it." Dani smiled at Cameron through a yawn, then shut her eyes and laid her head against the back of the love seat. But only for a moment. To rest. Then she'd go to bed.

Cameron squinted his eyes at the sunlight trickling in through the blinds at the front window. She wasn't exactly a dead weight, but Danica hadn't been as light as a feather either, twisted up like a pretzel all over him and sound asleep for four hours now. He hadn't found the heart to awaken her once she'd dozed off, but he hadn't expected her to make a night of it on top of him either. Apparently, he'd been wrong. She'd slept like a contented baby in some very nice positions, and some very difficult ones on him, and now he wasn't sure if his right leg and left shoulder had simply fallen off or were permanently damaged from the tingles shooting through them.

Yet he still didn't want to wake her up. Danica needed her sleep more than he needed his circulation. So, very carefully, he shifted himself under her, pushing her a little to the side of his aching scapula, and shut his eyes, wishing he were stretched out in a nice, comfy bed with her, instead of here on this seat from hell meant for two people—two who were sitting side by side, not stretched out, sleeping. Or, in his case, trying to sleep.

Cameron thought briefly about going to work, but then he remembered this was Saturday and his clinic was closed for regular appointments. Emergencies and extenuating circumstances only. Such a lax schedule compared to what he'd once had.

He'd once worked sixty hours a week minimum, most often a lot more, his clinic open all odd hours of the day and night. In an immediate care practice with his three partners, people had flocked in during those hours when they hadn't been able to see their own doctors, or when they'd wanted non-emergency treatment right away and their doctors hadn't been available. It had been a revolving-door medical practice where people had come and gone out, rarely ever returning. Impersonal, but necessary, as had been seen in the numbers of people coming in the door.

Impersonal had been fine, but cancer had a way of changing things, and one of the things that had changed for him was that he'd been left with little desire to stay impersonal in his practice. Life was too short to stay uninvolved. And in the oddest sort of way, this little practice he had going in Lexington…well, he wouldn't go so far as to say this was the dream of his heart, professionally speaking. But he also wouldn't say that it wasn't. In a lot of ways, he liked it, liked the offbeat people, liked the familiarity. In odd moments, he almost saw himself staying there. Very odd moments, he conceded.

After a few months of chemotherapy, he'd gotten to where he just hadn't been able to keep up the hectic pace at his old clinic, so he'd started cutting back his hours. Stopping altogether had been unthinkable, as had been ending his relationship with Sarah, even though he'd known both his professional and personal relationships had changed for the worse. But quitting on either had meant admitting something he hadn't wanted to admit, king of denial that he was. So he'd merely hung on, ignoring the obvious, until the obvious had become so glaringly large he'd no longer been able to ignore it. For the good of the clinic, he'd replaced himself with a full-time practitioner and gone on a long holiday, alone, to figure out what to do with his medical career and life in general.

Funny, that, how he'd gone from never wanting to be alone to craving it as part of his cure. His journey through cancer had taken a drastic turn the day he knew he *could* be alone, that for the sake of the things and people he did care about in his life he had to walk away from everything in order to find himself.

Serendipity struck fairly quickly after that, because within a month he found the ad in the medical journal offering a medical practice in a small village along a winding river. The exact pitch read, "A quiet, peaceful, relaxing medical practice in an idyllic setting along a river." Well, that sure sounded like heaven. Of course, his oncologist warned him to keep his activities limited for a while. So he took over the Lexington practice as a part-time endeavor, with the consent of its former doctor, and also with the understanding that he would either work up to a full-time practice eventually or turn it over to another doctor who would.

Full time here did sound appealing, but he wasn't ready to make a permanent decision yet. In so many ways he longed for his old schedule, but he liked what he had here. For now, though, he was just biding his time, waiting to see what his future held other than more of the uncomfortable pressure that Danica's knee was causing in his crotch. Time to wake her up, he decided as he gave her a gentle nudge.

"What?" she mumbled, her head buried in his neck.

Mercy, she smelled good. Her hair, her skin… His mind was toying on the edge of a fantasy where they were waking up together in a very different way. Dangerous fantasy. One in which he wasn't allowed. "Danica," he said, turning his head away from her so he wouldn't have to smell the jasmine in her hair. He loved jasmine…on her. "Time to wake up."

"Five more minutes," she begged.

In five more minutes he would have an erection that ached and a grisly mood that ached almost as badly. "Now," he said, giving her another nudge, this time successfully rolling some of her weight off him yet not pushing her all the way to the floor.

"In a minute." Her voice sounded like a purr, and as her knee moved away from the crucial area, Cameron did feel another pressure there, one he simply didn't want. He *could not* be attracted to her this way. He wouldn't let it happen.

Yet the erection straining at his pants was telling him something entirely different, betraying a part of him he'd put on hold until the rest of his life was back in order. "I've got to go," he said, but, dear lord, he didn't want to. "Get up, Danica. I've got to get going!" He gave her another little nudge, but this time she was half-awake and, perhaps, startled by where she found herself, because she lurched hard enough to send her falling to the floor.

Cameron immediately sat straight up and looked down at her as she opened her eyes and came to full awareness.

"Did we sleep together?" she asked right off.

"In a manner of speaking, I suppose you could say that we did." At least, she had. He'd spent most of his time thinking thoughts he shouldn't have and trying to make sure she was comfy. And regretting the fact that *thinking* was the only vice he allowed himself. At least, for now.

"On the love seat?"

He nodded, then stretched his stiffening neck back and forth, then in circles, to work out kinks that were only now becoming apparent to him.

"And I got the best of it, didn't I?" she asked, still sprawled flat.

"Depends on your definition of best. You got the sleep, I got the stiff muscles." He stretched out his arms then moved his shoulders in a circle. "But you were sleeping so well I didn't want to disturb you."

"You need to stretch out in a nice hot bath and soak for a while," she said quite pragmatically. "It's what I always did for my patients with stiff muscles. Works wonders."

"Your patients? As in...?"

"Dogs, mostly. People don't think their pets can get stiff muscles like people do, but they can, and so often when a dog pulls up lame, goes to walking on three legs rather than four, it's a good, stiff muscle pull. So, I installed a Jacuzzi in my office, and it's amazing what a nice soak can do to make things all better again." She smiled. "Even for a dog."

"So, you're diagnosing me like I'm a dog?"

"Cats don't get muscle pulls so much. And even when they do, they don't take to the water like dogs." She sat up, then brushed the hair back from her face. "So my prescription for you would be to go home, run a nice hot bath and soak in it for a while."

"Except I don't have a tub," he said, swinging his feet to the floor. His legs felt like tree trunks, they were so stiff and heavy. "And something about spending that kind of time standing in the shower until my muscles feel better seems like more effort than it's worth."

"I have a tub," she offered. "Nice old Victorian clawfoot upstairs. You're welcome to use it."

Admittedly, the more his muscles screamed, the better it sounded. Normally, he wouldn't have been so out of shape, but he'd had so little exercise lately and, at times, it showed. Like now. And in front of someone he didn't particularly care to have see him this way.

All that aside, the bath did sound good and sometimes pride wasn't worth the effort it took to put it on. Especially when his muscles were crying for the therapeutic prescription Danica used on dogs, and now on recovering doctors. "Maybe I'll take you up on the offer."

"Help yourself. It's up the stairs, second door on the left. Clean towels are in the linen closet."

She wrinkled up her nose, and smiled at him. He hadn't seen her smile much, and now it was so beautiful. It was almost like all the worry that was usually etched on her face had vanished. She did need to smile more, and even though he knew he shouldn't be thinking the thought, he did want to be the one to cause that smile if for no other reason than he knew what it was like to go so long without smiling. In his life there hadn't been much to smile about for a while, and he wanted better for her.

"The soap's rose-scented," she added. "I like florals. Sorry I don't have anything more…manly." Then she actually laughed. "Unless you want to use what I use on Dag. It's herbal. Good for the skin. Or a nice, shiny coat."

"First the lady prescribes a dog treatment, then she offers me dog soap." He stood up, then gave her a hand to help her off the floor. And felt a spark like he'd felt last night…a spark he didn't want to feel. A spark that was there nonetheless. He took a quick glance to see if she might have felt it, but she was simply staring at him, no discernible expression on her face. So maybe this was just an overreaction to some lusty thoughts. Lusty, indeed! Nothing like them had crossed his mind in a very long time, and even now, remembering, he was feeling the strain of an erection again.

Suddenly he felt like the thirteen-year-old boy at his first dance. The music is perfect for a slow dance, he places his hands, oh, so carefully in the right places on the girl, the two of them come together in real physical contact, start to dance, then…the embarrassment. It's right there, she can probably feel it poking at her and if she chances a look down she'll see the tell-tale signs of a teen-age boy's out-of-control arousal straining at his trousers. And all he can do is keep dancing, hoping his erection will go away by the time the music stops, and feel so red-faced through it all. "Thanks, but rose is fine," he said, hurrying off toward the stairs before she saw the red rising to his cheeks. And other parts on the rise again as well.

"Takes the water a few minutes to heat up," she called after him.

Hot water…actually, at that very moment, he was wondering if a nice cold shower wouldn't have been more appropriate.

A quick shower was fine enough for her. Thank heavens her sprawling Victorian had three bathrooms, and she was through with it, dressed, and fixing breakfast by the time Cameron came back downstairs. She really hadn't meant to simply collapse on him the way she had, and the least she could do for the poor man was fix him something to eat for his troubles. "I hope you like French toast," she said. She hadn't had it since before her accident. It had always been her favorite, and this morning she'd woken up practically craving it.

"You didn't have to," he said, walking into the kitchen.

His hair was wet—combed straight back and curling on the ends over the collar of his shirt. Even though his clothes were crumpled and he had a day's growth of dark stubble, it was such a sexy look on him. And those eyes…they were dark brown like his hair, with a slight twinkle to them. His smile was nice, too. A little crooked, but friendly, and sexy in a cute sort of way. The kind of smile that would immediately put someone at ease. *Or seduce them.* So many things she was noticing now that she'd been trying not to. "Well, actually, it's for me. But I couldn't possibly eat as much as I've fixed, and since you're here…"

He chuckled. "For a minute I thought you were going to tell me that I could have what your dog didn't want. Dog therapy, dog soap, dog scraps…"

"He does love French toast, too," she teased. "Grab a couple of plates from the cupboard and we'll eat here in the kitchen, if that's all right." The porch would have been nice, but somehow the coziness of her kitchen seemed better. More intimate, perhaps. "And thank you for letting me sleep. That's the longest I've slept since…" Since she'd been released from the hospital all those months ago. Then she'd gone into rehab, and that's where her nights had turned interminably long. She hadn't been able to lie in bed and do anything other than stare at the ceiling, and even to this day she could recite the number of ceilings tiles that tiny little room had.

After that, she'd gone to stay with Jason and Priscilla, friends from Global Response, and she'd spent many nights wandering around their ranch when sleep hadn't taken her. The same with her parents when she'd eventually ended up there…more sleepless nights. It had been no better when she'd finally gone to her own home either. "It was nice to have more than a couple of hours in a row," she said, taking the French toast off the griddle and placing it on a serving plate. "I think I've become a bit of an insomniac lately."

"If I were your doctor, I'd prescribe a sleeping pill."

She smiled. "Then it's a good thing you're not, because I wouldn't take it. After a year and a half of so many different drugs…" She shook her head. "I can manage without them."

"Sometimes your doctor does know best."

"And sometimes the patient knows best."

Cameron sat down at the round oak table and Dani took her place clear across on the other side, with an expanse of three chairs to her left and three to her right between them. It was a bit impersonal, but it was nice looking across at him. A very nice way to start the day, actually, even though she knew she had no right to enjoy his company.

"So what would you do with one of your patients who didn't follow your orders?" he asked.

"First, I'd bribe him with a doggie treat, maybe a bit of liver. It's amazing how well you can slip a pill into any number of things a dog likes to eat. Now, if it's a cat…"

He shook his head, smiling. "Is this your way of telling me it's none of my business?"

"No. It's my way of telling you they can send you home from the hospital with a whole pharmacy, but a pill's effect is only temporary, and it doesn't make the real pain go away, when what you need to deal with most are the emotional after-effects." So many of them in her case. "What I'm doing works, Cameron. A lot of people don't think it makes sense to ignore doctor's orders, but I do know my own capabilities and limitations better than anybody else, and it's working, I think. Perhaps taking longer this way, but I feel good about not curing myself with so many drugs."

"Strong lady," he commented.

She laughed. "Not always. Believe me, in the long, sleepless nights there are times I would take a sleeping pill if I kept them here. Which is why I don't."

"So what made you decide to become a veterinarian?" he asked. "Did you want to be a doctor?"

"I *am* a doctor," she said, defensively. "Of veterinary medicine. And in case you didn't know, it takes as long to become a veterinarian as it does a medical doctor. I love animals and it was always my first choice of career, and the only thing I ever wanted to do. People assume that if you can't get into medical school you automatically turn to dental school or veterinary school, but there are some of us who actually make those choices first. I love animals and it never occurred to me that I'd ever want a medical practice for anything other than dogs and cats. So what made you decide to become a medical doctor?" she countered, a slight smile tugging at her lips as she dragged a bite of French toast through a glop of maple syrup then watched the excess drip off. "Did you want to be a veterinarian and didn't make it to veterinarian school so you settled for medical school?"

He laughed. "Point taken, *Doctor*. And I apologize."

"Did I sound a little too defensive?"

"More like militant."

"Good. Like I said, I love being a veterinarian. Love my dogs and cats and various other four-legged critters. They're unassuming and accepting."

"And I love my two-legged patients, even though they're very assuming and rarely accepting," he said casually. "So you'll return to a vet practice eventually?"

She shrugged. "Probably, although I haven't thought much about it. Who knows? I could even stay right here in Lexington as there's no vet nearby…to take care of Amanda Milford's cats." He was asking personal questions, so now it was her turn to try again. "What about your practice, the one you left to come here? Have you thought about what you're going to do with it?"

"I still own a part interest in it. I just don't run it right now, so I turned the day-to-day activities over to my partners and for now I'm only a name at the top of the letterhead."

For now? Did that mean he wanted to return to his practice? This was curious, and she wanted to ask more, but he took a big bite of toast and now he was totally caught up in chewing. Also, he had another bite at the ready on his fork, so that was definitely his way of telling her he didn't want to talk about it and this was none of her business. They were friends, but only at an arm's length. Frustrating, to say the very least. The man was like a closed clam shell when it came to his life—a clam that just wouldn't be prised open. "Do you think we could call and see how Jeremy and Robby are doing?" Good, safe topic between them. Get off the personal, stay focused on the impersonal.

"I'm going to drive over this morning if you'd like to ride along and see for yourself."

She thought about it for a moment, and her first inclination was to decline. That was nearly a half-hour ride and she didn't feel comfortable doing it with him. But she did particularly want to see how Robby was doing. Poor child had lost his mother. He was probably scared to death in the hospital, not knowing anyone, not understanding anything that was happening, wondering why his mother wasn't coming to get him. She thought about some of the children she'd rescued on various callouts in the past, how terrified they'd been, and how the simple things had made them feel better—a stuffed animal, someone to hold them or read them a story. Robby needed that, and needed someone to tell him that everything would be fine, even though his world had just come crashing down around him.

"Could we stop somewhere so I can buy him a stuffed animal?"

"So, what made you decide you wanted a rescue dog?" Cameron asked as they entered the toy store parking lot.

There hadn't been much conversation between them on the drive. He seemed rather uneasy for some reason and, for her, that was fine. Breakfast had been nice, conversation pleasant and insignificant, and after that, as she'd said goodbye to him at the front door it had felt rather like a first date with its awkward, pregnant pause—to kiss, or not to kiss? Certainly, that hadn't been the emotion between them but, whatever it was, it had been strange. Strange and strained from the moment she'd asked about the medical practice until he'd left, actually. That did open things up to all kinds of speculations as he'd said he still owned the clinic. *Like, why had he left?* But she'd respected his distance as he had, so far, respected hers, so she hadn't asked. And now there was politeness between them, but not a relaxed one. Surprisingly, it felt a pity as she rather liked what was developing—liked the way she felt when he touched her. *As a friend, of course.*

"I decided I wanted a rescue dog after a friend of mine got into it. He was another vet from Purdue University, a classmate, and after he set up his veterinary practice, one of his first patients was a rescue dog. He was intrigued, and impressed, so he offered free care to rescue dogs. Shortly after that, he was asked to go out on a rescue to tend to the dogs. From there he got his own dog. She had puppies, and I took the pick of the litter. As it turned out, rescue is an instinct and Dag inherited it from his mother."

"But you're a paramedic."

"Seemed logical. Makes me better rounded and more useful, being able to take care of the dogs as well as the people we rescue. And, trust me, people are much easier about being treated by a paramedic than a vet, although, to be honest, the skills a veterinarian uses on an animal patient aren't much different than the skills required for a human patient. Different proportions, usually the same techniques and medicines for the same effects overall. But when you're out saving someone like Jeremy Lawson, who trusts you to save him, you're probably better off not letting him know your first line of medical practice is small animals and that what you're doing for him is much the same thing you'd do for a French poodle."

Once the car came to a stop, Dani hopped out. "This won't take long," she said as she shut the door. She thought about asking Cameron to come along, but with his somber mood this morning she wasn't sure he would want to. So she hurried into the store, figuring if he wanted to follow her, he would.

Which turned out to be the case. Before she'd reached the

aisle with all the stuffed toys, Cameron caught up with her. "Find one that's hypo-allergenic," he said. "We don't know if he has allergies."

"I wouldn't have thought about that," she commented, picking up a little blue elephant, looking at the tag, then putting it down again. "I suppose I always thought stuffed toys were stuffed toys."

He chuckled. "Not all created equal." He glanced at the tag of a green frog wearing a red and yellow vest, then shoved it back on the shelf.

"I suppose being a people doctor has some advantages. I mean, my recommendation would go more toward buying a natural product, one without artificial additives and chemicals, as my patients pretty much always chew up their toys."

"Then we're not that unalike. I like natural, too. And some of my younger patients do chew." He tossed a cotton teddy bear at Dani. "But you've got to also consider choking hazards like eyes that might come off and pop into a child's mouth, buttons, snaps, or even a tail that could be pulled off."

"You're not a father, are you?" she asked, satisfied that Cameron's bear was perfect...hypo-allergenic, no eyes, tails, buttons or snaps that could come off. And the tag read for ages three and under.

"Definitely not a father. Lots of nieces and nephews, but that's as far as it goes."

He should have his own children, she thought. He had that quality about him—the kind a child would be drawn to. The kind that, in spite of all her hard attempts not to get too involved with him, was getting her involved.

Friendship, she reminded herself. That's all.

But when she watched him pick up a couple of story books for Robby, a longing such as she'd never felt in her life congealed like a lump in her stomach, and her heart lurched.

Cameron would be a beautiful father someday. And she desperately wanted to be a mother.

As she walked to the checkout, clutching the bear to her chest, she brushed back a tear sliding down her cheek. One of life's bitter ironies—when she could have had children she hadn't been ready, and now, as she was discovering she was ready, she couldn't.

She glanced back at Cameron as he came up behind her in line, his arms full of more toys for Robby. Yes, he would make a beautiful father.

CHAPTER SIX

CAMERON stood in the hall, looking in through the pediatric observation window at Danica. She'd been sitting in the rocking chair for an hour now, talking to Robby, even though the instant she'd picked him up he'd nestled in, all snuggled with his new stuffed teddy bear, and gone right to sleep. According to the nursing notes, he'd had a restless night, crying intermittently for his mother. Then Danica had come, the balm he needed.

She glanced through the window and smiled back at Cameron, and he was stunned by the beauty of that picture—Danica holding the boy in her arms. Had she ever wanted to be a mother? Maybe with Tom? She would have been a natural at it, he thought. Good with little boys, good with animals…it was nice to see her step out of her overwhelming situation for a little while to become the person he knew she should be.

"Dr. Enderlein?" an older man enquired, stepping out from behind the nurses' desk, extending his hand in greeting. "I'm Dr. Wallace, the staff pediatrician here. I've been tending Robby since he was admitted last night, and I've been told you were the admitting physician."

"I am. I brought him in after the accident, and he seems no worse for his trauma," Cameron said, shaking the man's hand. "I was the family physician."

Dr. Wallace was a kindly-looking man, a grandfather type with silver-gray hair, bushy eyebrows and a pot belly. "I'm sorry to hear about his mother. That's going to be tough on him. But physically Robby's fine. And I'd say he was a lucky little boy, being found the way he was."

Cameron cringed, thinking of how close Robby had come to not being found. If Dag hadn't jumped into the police car, if Danica hadn't come in after him…God knew what would have happened to the child. "The police officers on the scene speculate that he wasn't fastened into his seat belt and he was thrown free of the car. They think he might have unfastened himself and his mother was trying to get him back into his child seat when she swerved across the line and hit an oncoming car. And you're right. He was one very lucky child." Thanks only to Danica.

"Well, I know you'd told the nurses about his family situation, so I've had our social workers looking all morning for other family members. Unfortunately, at this point, the news isn't good."

"No one?" Cameron asked, suddenly concerned.

"Not yet, but we're still trying. The only problem is, he doesn't need to be here. We don't have a bed shortage in Pediatrics at the moment, but if that happens we'll have to discharge him."

"To where?" Cameron asked, although he already knew the answer. Knew it, and didn't like it.

"Foster-care, if we have a foster-parents available. If not, to the guardian home."

"An institution," Cameron said, his voice flat.

"For now. A child his age usually gets foster-parents in a matter of weeks, though. We keep them high on our priority list, and since children are always entering and leaving the system, we've got a pretty good success record of securing satisfactory placement."

Satisfactory placement. Such an impersonal situation for Robby. "And what do you consider satisfactory?"

"Someone who will provide a safe environment and attend to all the child's physical needs."

"And a child like Robby, who's just lost his mother, what do you do for someone like him?"

Dr. Wallace cocked an inquisitive eyebrow. "As much as we can, but the system's not perfect. And you've got to keep in mind that while foster-parents fulfill a need, and for the most part they do care about their charges, it's only a temporary home until something better comes along. Often they care for several children at a time, which means each child might not get the personal attention they need but they will receive the basics. It's not the same thing as being in a real home."

"Impersonal," Cameron said.

"Sometimes."

"But if you don't have an opening in a foster-home right now…"

"Then like I said, he'll go to the guardian home."

"Even more impersonal."

"Unfortunately, yes."

"I know that child, knew his mother. She wouldn't have wanted—"

"But she doesn't have a choice in it now, does she?"

Cameron shut his eyes for a moment, trying to picture Robby in a institution, or even in a foster-home. "He has a peanut allergy. *A serious one.*"

"We'll note that appropriately on his chart."

"But in an institution it could get overlooked."

"Like I said, it's not perfect. We do our best, and that's all I can promise you."

"He's also prone to ear infections. They're not always symptomatic."

"So, what are you suggesting here, Doctor?" A cagy smile crept to Dr. Wallace's lips. "That you take the boy home with you until we can find a permanent situation for him?"

"Is that what you think I'm suggesting?"

"If it isn't, you should be."

"But I work."

"So do many parents."

"And I'm single."

"So was his mother, according to the chart, and she managed. It's a modern world, Doctor. Single working parents do a good job of raising children these days. Besides, this would only be a temporary situation."

"I don't know how long I'll be staying in Lexington."

"And I don't know how long I'd be leaving Robby in your care."

"You can do that? Make the decision?"

"I'm director of the board that governs the guardian home. That earns me some privileges."

"Don't your foster-parents have to have some training?" It was absolutely incredible that he would even entertain the notion of taking care of Robby, but that's exactly what he was doing. He wasn't sure why except that it was personal, he knew the child, knew how much Robby's mother had loved him, and in an odd way he felt drawn to do this.

"Usually, but you're the child's physician, you have a history with him, and you obviously have his best interests at heart. And I know for a fact that at the guardian home, peanut butter and jelly sandwiches are a staple food. If you take Robby with you, you won't have to worry that he'll have a bad reaction if he accidentally gets some peanut butter because you'll see to it he doesn't get into it."

Cameron gave his head an amazed shake. "It sure wasn't what I'd expected when I got up this morning."

"Life has a way of throwing us those surprises when we least expect them, doesn't it?" Dr. Wallace said, giving Cameron a cordial slap on the back. "But sometimes they work out."

"How long can he stay here? It looks like I may have some arrangements to make."

"Two days at the longest. If we need the bed, sooner. And we won't stop looking for a relative to take him, in the meantime."

Cameron knew the next words from his mouth would be an acceptance. He was about to agree to being a foster-parent— someone who took temporary custody. Cameron Enderlein, foster-father. It did have a nice ring to it, didn't it?

"So?" Dr. Wallace prodded.

Cameron glanced over his shoulder at Danica in time to see her place a tender kiss on Robby's cheek. Then he smiled. "So, yes. I'll do it. I'll take Robby for now, because I think I've just figured out how I'm going to manage it."

"I know the pain," she whispered, even though Robby was fast asleep. "I know how badly it's going to hurt you, and if I could, I'd take it all away from you…protect you from the bad things." Sadly, even at his young age, he couldn't be shielded, and that broke her heart. Who would hold him when he cried? Wipe his tears? Whisper the things to him that a mother would whisper to comfort her child?

Who would love him the way only a mother could love her child?

"I can see why your mother did what she did in order to have you," Dani whispered to the sleeping boy, as she cuddled him a little closer. "You were so loved, Robby. More than you can probably ever understand, somebody loved you more than anything else in this world, and in the days and weeks and months ahead when you'll need it most, I hope somebody will tell you that every day. You need to know. We all need to know that we're loved, that when someone we love goes away, the love doesn't end. I hope someone will love you enough to teach you that because, in the end, that's all we have, Robby. The love is all we really have." She glanced out the observation window at Cameron, who was talking to Robby's pediatrician. "All any of us really need."

A contented sigh escaped Dani's lips as she pulled the fuzzy blue blanket up over Robby's shoulders. "Your child will be taken care of, Linda," she whispered. "I'm so sorry you won't be the one here to do it but I promise you, your child will be taken care of. And loved." She didn't know how it would happen. She only knew it would.

As days went, this one was nice. Nice sun, unseasonably warm for this early in the spring. Dani relaxed pleasantly into the car seat and stared out the window at the passing scenery. Houses, businesses, patches of empty land floated by for the first few miles of the ride back home, then the landscape turned into nothing but budding trees and bushes and blossoming spring flowers on one side of the road, with the long stretch of lazy river on the other, all the way to Lexington.

As a young girl she'd always loved this drive, always pretended it was something much more exotic and exciting than it really was. In a child's mind, the river was the ocean, the barges traveling up and down it mighty ships on their way to mysterious foreign ports. The trees and flowers along the road were a vast, untamed jungle to explore. So many possibilities for a child.

Dani remembered her grandmother's stories of pirate adventures on the river and jungle explorers in the woods. To a small child, they had been wild and exciting tales that had been so real to her she'd always looked for those pirates and explorers. Of course, as she'd gotten older she'd known better. In a way, that was sad as those imaginary adventures had been an important part of growing up that she'd enjoyed so much. For some reason, today she was looking out the window for those pirates and explorers. Not in a literal sense, of course, but in a way Robby might look for them with the awe only a child could have—if she had the chance to tell him those stories, which she probably would not. "You've been awfully quiet," she finally said to Cameron after nearly ten minutes of total silence between them. What kind of stories were going on in his mind in all that empty time? she wondered.

"Thinking about things I've done, things maybe I shouldn't have done."

He'd been oddly quiet and withdrawn, even for him, since they'd left the hospital. His two patients there were coming along nicely—Robby in almost perfect condition, and Jeremy healing better than expected for someone who'd just had a hole poked into his lung. So what had made Cameron so melancholy? "Anything you want to talk about?" she prompted, not sure she should have. But being with Cameron while he was in this mood didn't seem right. Normally, he was the one coaxing her to talk or be more outgoing. Had he learned something about one of his two patients that worried him? Something he wasn't telling her? "It's not Robby or Jeremy, is it?"

"No, they're fine," he said. "Physically, they're coming along well."

What was it, then? Dani wondered as she sat another five minutes, staring out the window, listening again to the total quiet between them. There was definitely something going on with him, and she was feeling some concern over it.

"Look, Cameron, you've been trying to be a friend to me ever since I've been here and I've been resisting that pretty much every time you made an effort. But I do appreciate it. I want you to know that." Maybe that would start something. She hoped it would anyway, but one look at him revealed that his face was still fixed in the same tight frown it had been since they'd left the hospital, and he was concentrating so hard on the road ahead she wasn't sure he'd even heard her. "And I'd like to be your friend," she continued. "Unless I've already burned that bridge."

Again, a quick glance at his face revealed nothing. The man was a virtual stone and because he wasn't responding she was beginning to wonder if she had, indeed, burned her bridges with him where friendship was concerned. She couldn't blame him, really, with the way she'd put him off. Admittedly, she was disappointed. In fact, more disappointed than she'd expected to be. "So if there's anything you'd like to talk about…something going on that maybe I could help you with…"

Nice try, but no response from him this time either, and Dani was finally becoming irritated. Could this be his way of giving her what she'd given him at the start of the relationship—cold indifference? Somehow, she didn't think so. Cameron didn't seem the type to act that way. Which meant something *was* bothering him. Something that had started at the hospital. *Or with her.* "Just tell me what it is!" she said in more of a huff than she'd intended. In fact, she'd huffed it out in a way that made her sound like she actually cared. Perhaps she did a little. In a no-strings-attached kind of casual way, she did like Cameron, and right now something was pushing her to be the friend to him he'd been trying to be to her. "If it's something I've done, I have the right to know."

"It's…complicated, and I'm not sure you're ready to get involved in what I seem to have gotten us involved in."

"Tell me what it is and I'll tell you if I'm ready to get involved in it."

"I'm going to be taking custody of Robby for a little while, until a relative can be found or other arrangements can be made."

"I…I'm not exactly speechless, but I didn't expect *you* to volunteer for something like this. I mean, how can you—?"

"Take care of a child? Darned if I know. At the time it seemed like the right thing to do, but now that I've had some time to think about it I'm not sure how I'm going to manage."

"So, why?" she asked.

"I suppose because as bumbling as I'm going to be at doing this, I didn't want Robby going to an institution, which is where he'd have probably gone. I was his mother's doctor, and I'm his doctor. When I thought about him and all the things that could happen…he has a peanut allergy and all they give them to eat is peanut butter. So what happens if he accidentally gets into it? That could happen as they've got so many children to look after. He's also prone to asymptomatic ear infections, and what happens if he's sick and no one notices?"

"So you volunteered because you'll do a better job taking care of him," she said softly. Indeed, a beautiful father.

"Yeah," Cameron snorted, "like I really know how to take care of a child."

"It's not about what you know, Cameron. It's about what you feel."

"Well, right now I'm feeling a little nauseated. It's a crazy idea. I work during the day, I get called out to emergencies…"

"And you'll be good with him, no matter how you work it out."

"How I work it out… My first thought was to have him at the office with me, perhaps turn the storage room into a play room. But that still doesn't take care of emergencies when I get called out at night. I can't drag him out to those. And even at the office I'll be busy most of the time, and he's too young to be left on his own, even while I'm there. It's too dangerous."

"Then I can take care of him," she offered immediately. Suddenly, she was excited. Out of the blue, with never a thought in her head that something like this could happen, it was already what she wanted to do more than anything else in the world. "For emergencies, too," she added. "And instead of taking him to the office, you can leave him at my house during those few hours every day. There's an attic full of old toys my sister and I had when we were young, and the swing is still in the tree in the back yard. I think he might enjoy it there." A picture of Robby playing in that swing came to mind, and immediately Cameron stepped into that picture to give Robby a push. It was a happy, cozy scene, and one she had no to right to. But it was like a snapshot. Once taken, it wasn't going to be gotten rid of so easily.

"Actually, I'd thought along those lines when I'd volunteered to keep him. But then I started wondering if you were up to it. I mean, you're not exactly pushing yourself very hard to get over your accident. You've come a little way, yet you're still resistant to so many things, and putting Robby into the middle of that worries me because, honestly, the boy needs more than spending every morning on the front porch wrapped in a quilt while drinking tea and staring across the road at the river."

Dani twisted in the seat to face him directly. "Do you really think that's the way I'd treat a little boy?" she snapped.

Cameron shrugged. "Maybe you wouldn't intend to, but I think it would become a very easy thing for you to do."

"I'm not so self-absorbed, Cameron. I'm recovering from a trauma and a tragedy, but I'm not an idiot. I know a child like Robby needs stimulation—activity, education, all kinds of things to occupy his day other than quilts and tea on the porch. And I'm really offended that you think I'd treat him that way!"

"It's not what I think you'd do. Not intentionally. But what happens when you get up one morning and you're not feeling up to what it takes to take care of a little boy? What will you do then?"

They pulled to a stop at a four-way in the main intersection of Lexington, and without thinking about it, Dani opened the car door and jumped out.

"What the hell are you doing?" Cameron shouted at her.

"Walking. I feel the urge for tea and quilts coming on and I certainly don't want to do it in your car." With that, she slammed the door, ran to the sidewalk, and started walking. By the time she reached the end of the block, Cameron had already driven ahead of her. Now she didn't see him. And she didn't care. What he'd said had been uncalled for. And cruel. She did have what it took to take care of a child for a few hours a day, and she wasn't so deep in a slump that she'd pull Robby in with her. If he was in her care, he was her priority. There were no two ways about that. But Cameron actually thought she'd be so self-centered she wouldn't do a good job with the boy, and that wasn't true. She wanted to take care of him.

Cameron doubted her, though, and she didn't know if she was more hurt than angry, or angry than hurt. Didn't matter. Either way, Cameron didn't trust her, which meant he wouldn't let her near Robby.

So much for her budding friendship with the good doctor, she thought as she marched straight by his medical office. And so much for pirate adventures and jungle explorers with Robby.

Pausing, Dani read the gold-printed name on the window. DR CAMERON ENDERLEIN, MD. "Well, Doctor," she snapped. "Looks like we won't be enjoying Nora Carston's cinnamon buns together in the near future." Strangely, that pronouncement came with a lump in her throat. Disappointment? Or some leftover anger? Whatever the case, it didn't matter. Dani picked up her pace, determined to get home and slam a door or two in a good case of outrage. Then pretend Cameron Enderlein had never entered her life. Which wouldn't be easy because she actually did like the little spot he took up there.

"Well, she's certainly got a temper," Cameron said to himself. He chuckled, watching her in his rear-view mirror as she stomped her way up the little hill on her way home. He hadn't meant to be cruel, but in a sense he did have to find out what she had in her if she were to take over part of the care for Robby, and this was perfect. It told him a lot. She wasn't all flat inside like she put on. She had some passion, some emotion left for something she really cared for. Watching her sit in the rocking chair, holding Robby in her arms as she had, he'd really hoped something was sparking there. Deep down he'd felt it was, and now he was glad he was right about it.

Actually, she might have been the perfect one to take over total guardianship of Robby in the short term, except Dr. Wallace had said he was given some latitude in the decision to bend the rules, but not all that much. Sending a child home with the child's physician wouldn't raise much question, he'd said. However, when Cameron had asked if Danica might be considered for the position instead of him, Wallace had merely shaken his head. He knew Danica, knew her current situation and didn't think she was ready yet for all that responsibility. Under Cameron's watchful eye she would be allowed to help care for Robby, but not otherwise.

Meaning he was the one. The only one. And that did scare him… The more he thought about it, the more frightened he became of the responsibility. Certainly, he knew how to treat a child medically, how to look for illnesses, bandage a cut or a scrape, set a broken arm. *Protect a child from a peanut allergy and ear infections.* Those were doctor things, though, but in all likelihood he'd be in the position to do daddy things in a few days, which was an entirely different set of circumstances. So while he'd been busy questioning Danica's abilities to help with Robby on a part-time basis, he probably should have been questioning his own to take care of the child on a full-time basis. "I'm going to need lots of help," he said on a sigh as he opened the car door and got ready to step out and stop Danica's march toward home.

"Leave me alone!" she snapped at him before he was fully out of the car. She didn't even slow down.

"We need to talk, Danica."

"We have. You've said everything you need to."

He hurried to catch up, then he fell in step along side her as she entered her front gate and headed for the porch. "Not everything. All those things I said—"

"You meant them," she interrupted, thumping up the steps.

"It was a concern. I'll admit that."

"Your concern, but none of my concern."

Dani pulled open the screen door and started to twist the doorknob, but Cameron pulled the screen door back even further and stepped around in front of her to block her from going inside. Once she was in, she'd slam the door in his face. He knew that, and he also knew that it might be a long time before she ever came out again. Or ever spoke to him again. *Thanks to all those stupid things he'd said.* Well, he wasn't about to let that happen. "Look, Danica, I've never taken care of a child, and if you're to do that with me, and I hope you will, I have the right to worry about how you'll handle it. That's all it was about. It wasn't personal and I didn't mean to hurt you, but I had to be honest."

"If I'm to do that with you? First, you presume to include me in that arrangement of yours without consulting me. And you admitted as much. Then, when I agree to help, you question my abilities and imply…no, not even imply. You simply state I'll allow my problems to interfere with caring for Robby, which is ridiculous. I'm a trained veterinarian, Cameron. My job is to nurture and care for creatures, and I do it because I love caring for those who can't care for themselves. Granted, in your opinion I only take care of animals, but I'm not some bone-lazy, do-nothing mass of self-pity who'll let my problems come first where Robby is concerned. That's not who I am, and under no circumstances is that what I ever do. You don't know me, and you had no right to say it. Now, get out of my way."

He liked that spark in her. Actually, it was a whole lot more than a spark. It was a full flame, and it was sizzling hot right now. Granted, that heat was directed right at him, and not in a good way. But he was happy to see it because now he had no doubts about her whatsoever. She would give Robby everything she had and everything he needed, and make up for the things *he* didn't even begin to know how to give the child. Danica was a natural, a mother not yet graced with a child. Robby was a child not now graced with a mother.

This would be as good for Danica as it would be for Robby. In a way he'd never expected, he was glad to be part of it. "Can I come in for a cup of tea?" he asked. "And an opinion on how to set up a bedroom for a little boy?"

"I haven't agreed to do this."

"Sure you did, a few minutes ago in the car."

"If you recall, you didn't want me."

"Danica, from the moment the idea entered my head I knew I wanted you to help. But I had to be honest with you. Among all my own self-doubts over doing this, I did have concerns about you, too, and you'll have to admit they're legitimate. This little boy is going to need so much from both of us, and what we're about to do…well, given my experience with child-rearing, I probably shouldn't have volunteered but Robby deserves better than he would have had otherwise."

"It doesn't take experience, Cameron." Dani stepped around Cameron and entered the house, not objecting when he followed her in. "All it takes is heart." She turned to face him. "Yours is a little bit buried, but it's good."

She was right. His heart was a little bit buried. Problem was, Danica was disinterring it a little at a time, and there was nothing in him to resist that. Nothing at all.

"OK, so I probably shouldn't have gotten involved." Dani had been pacing the floor ever since her grandmother had arrived.

In a phone call, she'd mentioned in passing that she would be helping Cameron take care of a little boy, and Louise had immediately quit her golf game and come running. "But I did. And I'm not going to ask out of it now. Cameron's counting on me, and that little boy deserves better than sitting in an institution, waiting for a permanent home."

"You may want to do it, Dani, but are you up to it?" Louise asked quite simply. She was a bleached-blonde bombshell who still turned a lot of male heads, and without a wrinkle on her face she didn't come close to looking like Dani's grandmother. More like her mother. "If I'm not mistaken, it was only a couple of weeks ago that you wouldn't even open up the curtains and have a look outside, yet now you've not only gone out the door, you're in the process of dragging a child home with you. And to be honest, I'm worried about that. Not about your ability to take care of the boy, because I know you'll do a wonderful job there. But about how you'll take care of yourself while you're doing it. In case you haven't noticed, you don't always take good care of yourself these days, and it seems you always have an excuse. So I'm afraid this little boy might become a convenient excuse for you to use to neglect yourself."

"You, and Cameron! He said the same thing, in a roundabout way. He wanted me to help him yet he doubted that I could."

"He had a right to. You can be pretty stubborn, you know. And I'm sure Albert Wallace was pretty strict with the guidelines Cameron has to follow in order to keep the boy. Which is probably another of Cameron's concerns." She was referring to the doctor who would ultimately allow Cameron to take custody. He was one of Louise's oldest friends, and he'd called her about the plan for Dani to care part time for the child after Cameron had discussed it with him.

"It's not about Dr. Wallace's concern. That doesn't bother me."

A sly smile slid easily over Louise's face as she reached for the margarita pitcher to refresh her drink. They were in the enclosed veranda at the rear of the house, Louise stretched out in a lounge chair, sipping the rather strong drink she'd made for them, while Dani continued to pace back and forth, jiggling ice cubes in an empty glass of water. "Then that means it's about Dr. Enderlein. Rather a strong reaction, don't you think? The man doesn't know you, and he does have a right to be concerned."

"It's not his concern that worries me, either. It's—"

"The tie that binds?" Louise interrupted, turning a sympathetic look toward her granddaughter. "That's it, isn't it?"

"Meaning?"

"The little boy. Won't he tie you and Cameron together in a way you're not ready for yet?"

"We won't be tied together," Dani denied, then immediately changed her mind. "Well, maybe loosely. But not personally."

"The child makes it personal, Dani. Deny it all you want, but two people caring for one child makes the relationship *very* personal. You're worried because you think Tom wouldn't want that. In a way, that would be letting him go in ways you haven't been able to do yet."

Dani stopped her pacing and spun to face her grandmother. At first she didn't say anything. She simply stood there, too stunned to speak.

"It's true isn't it? You've put your life on hold because you don't think Tom would want you to go on. I know that sounds cruel, sweetie, and I really don't mean to be, but people lose loved ones every day and eventually they do go on. I did the same after your grandfather died. I sat on this very front porch every day much the same way you're doing, trying to hang onto him. It felt disloyal to his memory to go on, so I didn't. Not for a very long time."

Dani remembered that time. The spark in her grandmother had virtually died and, yes, she had huddled under a blanket on the front porch, staring out at the river. It had been a sad time for everyone. "What got you through?"

"Honestly, boredom was a big part of it. But I also thought about what your grandfather would have wanted, and he always liked the way I was active. He would have hated me doing pretty much what you've been doing—hiding away. And what I discovered was that once I started getting involved in life again—going places, meeting people—it didn't seem as disloyal as I thought it would. It didn't mean that my feelings for your grandfather were any less, because they weren't. It meant that my life was moving in new directions. I'll admit, it was tough at first. But it got easier. And it will for you, too, once you've decided to go on with your life. And Tom will stay with you, *in the right place,* just like your grandfather has always stayed with me. I promise you that, Dani."

"But I've gone on," Dani defended.

"Have you really? You've moved in a different direction, but are you really that far away from the accident and Tom's death, or are you circling it in different ways? I mean, Cameron's a nice man. A dedicated doctor. Very compassionate. And the two of you are about to take on the raising of a little boy, even if only for a little while. Yet here you are, pacing back and forth in some kind of panic because this is going to put you in close, constant contact with Cameron. And I suspect you're feeling guilty over that, which can only mean one thing. Are you developing feelings for him?"

For the second time in a minute her grandmother had left her speechless. There was no way to defend herself, no way to express her feelings because her grandmother had already made up her mind. "What I'm developing is a headache," she snapped, and that wasn't altogether untrue. A tiny throbbing was developing dead center in her forehead and zinging right into the back of her head. "I need an aspirin."

"You need a date. You need to admit that you like the man. Or that you're attracted to him. Or that you'd just like to sleep with him."

Twice speechless, and now the third time. There was no stopping her grandmother today. She was on a roll and, honestly, Dani just wasn't in the mood to do this. Not now. She'd spent the afternoon with Cameron, going over plans to bring Robby here, and with each and every passing minute the idea that this was going to be a huge mistake poked its way in even more. Because, yes, she did enjoy his company. And, yes, she did feel disloyal to Tom. Two feelings she couldn't reconcile with each other. "I need a nap," she lied, instead of arguing with her grandmother. "A long nap."

"You need a life, Dani. Running off and taking a nap isn't going to give you what you need, and you know that."

Dani slapped her hands on her hips in frustration. "So what do you want me to admit? That I like Cameron Enderlein? Yes, I do. And do you want me to admit that I'd like to sleep with him?" Dear God, where had that come from? She'd never, ever thought about sleeping with Cameron. Yet now that her grandmother had brought it up, that's all she had on her mind and she couldn't blink it away. Hidden desires? She didn't think so. Maybe it was just a longing to be held by someone again, to feel strong arms around her. To relax into an embrace and feel a sense of for ever there. Or maybe…no, she wasn't having *that* kind of physical urge. Hadn't had for so long. "No, I don't want to sleep with him." She'd barely had time enough to make love to Tom before he'd died. A few sporadic weeks had been all they'd had together and, yes, she felt cheated over that. There should have been more…should have been more time. "I don't want that kind of relationship with anybody," she said, her voice quivering. "I don't think I could ever do that again."

Immediately, Louise jumped up, ran to her granddaughter

and pulled her into her arms. "You'll want it when it's right, sweetie," she whispered. "And Tom would want it for you. He was a special young man who wouldn't like you spending your life grieving over him."

"He was special," Dani whispered, sniffling.

"And so is Cameron. Maybe not in the way Tom was special to you, but let him in, Dani. You're both about to take on a responsibility that's bigger than any of the reasons you have to stay away from him."

"I know," she said. Her eyes shut, she tried to conjure up Tom's image. It always calmed her, but this time, for a flash, it wasn't there to be conjured up. Cameron's was, though. His image appeared first, then came Tom's, and that brought a lump to her throat. "And so you'll know, under different circumstances Cameron and I…" She couldn't even say the words, because there were no circumstances different enough. "We're friends," she finally conceded. A friend whose image had just, again, pushed away the image of the man she would have married. That had happened twice in a minute and she wasn't sure what to make of it other than the fact that she was suddenly feeling queasy and light-headed. "I really do need that nap," she said. This time she meant it.

CHAPTER SEVEN

IT WAS quite strange, being out this early in the day. She wasn't just sitting on her front porch, gazing at the river, as she usually did. She was out walking down the main street in Lexington and not seriously nervous about it. A little nervous, of course. But the butterflies in her stomach were merely fluttering, not pounding.

Dani smiled, pleased with this bit of progress, even though she'd had to force herself to get to this point—a little self-nagging a while ago when she'd dawdled too long in the shower, then some scolding at the closet when she had been un-decided between the green and the peach T-shirts. Obviously, she had been stalling. She'd known that, and once she had filled her mind with what she was going to do this morning *for Robby,* her pace had picked up some. Admittedly, though, she'd almost gone into a quickstep when she'd thought about meeting Cameron. For whatever reason, he was her literal bump out the front door and her prod to the front walk and on out the rusty gate to the street.

So why the interest?

She did like him. More than that, she liked being with him. Maybe this new attitude was simply a need for some adult companionship. Heaven only knew, she'd shut herself off from it all this time. In the hospital, in the rehab center, staying with family and friends, she'd shut herself off completely from everything. So, yes, that had to be it! She needed adult companionship. That's why her pulse was quickening just the slightest, thinking about him. Cameron was a step back into the real world for her.

On her way by Nora Carston's bakery, Dani glanced in the window at the lovely pastries on display. Nora knew how to arrange them to make them tempting, and she couldn't resist, so she ducked inside, amid the wonderful smells wafting out from the kitchen and the friendly jingling of the bells on the door.

"Dani!" Nora cried, running around the counter to greet her with a hug. "How have you been?"

"Getting better," she said. "It takes time, but I'm coming along."

"I hear that you and that handsome doctor are about to start raising a child together. That little boy you found during that awful accident?"

That statement turned a few heads in the waiting line. "Not raise him. We're going to care for him until he has a permanent home. They wanted to send him to an institution and Cameron volunteered to keep him for a while, and I'm going to help while Cameron's at work. That's all it is."

"Well, it's a generous thing you're doing, Dani. I know you've had a tough time of it lately, but I think this will be good for you. It's about time you had a boyfriend again, too, and we all love Dr. Enderlein."

"But I don't…" Her words were cut off by the jingling bell over Nora's door, and the old woman flit away, leaving Dani alone with a mouthful of denials she wished she could have gotten out—especially when she turned around, bag of cinnamon buns in hand, to see a whole long line of smiling faces…every last one of them smiling right at her. Not one of them a stranger either. And all of them probably thinking to themselves what Nora had said out loud. "We're not…" she

said, then decided it best to simply let it go. The more she tried
to deny it, the more people would believe. As the last thing she
wanted was a rumor floating around about how she protested
too much over the mention of a relationship with Cameron, she
smiled, offered her goodbyes then scampered out the door,
with the distinct feeling that all eyes in the cozy bakery were
on her, and once the door was firmly shut, all tongues would
be wagging. About her, of course.

Didn't matter anyway. Actions spoke louder than words,
and there weren't going to be any actions to back up the
words. She hoped.

Or, did she?

"Robby had a good night," Cameron said, opening the door for
her. "I called the hospital and he's doing fine. So is Jeremy. He's
already up and walking around and anxious to get back to
school. They're probably going to release him in the next
couple of days."

Dani dropped the bag of buns on the reception desk and took
a good look around the office. It was her first time in and she
was amazed by how cluttered and cramped it was. Somehow
she'd imagined something very different—something more
tidy and efficient. But the waiting area here was small, with
barely enough room for four chairs, overflowing boxes of
children's toys, books, magazines stashed in every conceivable
open space, a television blaring away with the morning news
and…a piano? "Why the piano?" she asked.

"In case someone wants to play."

She blinked over that answer. In a skewed sort of way, it did
make sense. If someone wanted to play, there it was. But who
in their right mind went to a doctor's office to play the piano?

"It was here when I moved in," he continued. "Didn't see
any point in moving it."

"Are your examining rooms this cluttered?" she asked, heading down the hall to the first door. It was his office, a tiny, cramped closet of an area that looked much the same as the outer office, only smaller and with twice as much stuff in it. "No piano in here?" she asked, admittedly a bit shocked over the disarray in this part of Cameron's life.

He chuckled. "Actually, I did find a rusty trombone. It's in the storage room. They said this was a music studio before I took it over."

"So what ever possessed you to think you could turn it into a doctor's office?"

He shrugged, grinning. "It was cheap. Practically free since no one has rented it for years."

"Well, I don't suppose it's very wise to pass up cheap," she said, wondering if this was more about his lack of permanence here than anything else. Why bother setting up in a nice office if you don't intend to stay very long? Which, from all indications she'd seen so far, Cameron did not.

It did make her wonder how long he would stay here for Robby. She thought about asking, and decided it really wasn't any of her business what he did. Staying…leaving. Didn't matter. Nothing was permanent anyway, not even the things you counted on to be permanent.

"It looks like this is an exam room," she said, opening the door and nearly gasping at the small size of it. There was an exam table, a sink and a rolling stool. Nothing else. No room for it. Definitely not a situation for the long term. The jolt hit again when she peeked into the next exam room. It was like the first. Too small. Too impermanent. So was the storage room, which he hadn't even bothered to clean out from the previous tenant. All in all, there were so many answers here to questions she didn't dare ask because asking got her involved, and getting involved only hurt when someone went away.

Cameron meant to go away.

"It was here when I moved in," Cameron said, stepping up behind her as she stared into the cluttered store room. "I haven't had time to move everything out and get it organized."

"No, I don't suppose you have," she said, surprised by how heavy her words felt. The weight of them almost turned into a physical ache, and the implication did turn into panic. Was she falling in love with Cameron, as her grandmother had practically suggested?

That simply couldn't be, not after she'd promised herself she wouldn't. Yet thinking that did cause her heart to gallop and her breaths to go shallow. This wasn't what she wanted. *Not at all.* "Why are you doing this to Lexington?" she asked, looking for a way out of her thoughts.

"Doing what?"

"Leading them to believe you're their doctor, when you know in your heart that you're not. They're becoming dependent on you, Cameron. People in small towns do that." *She was doing that.* "You become part of them and they trust you to be there when they need you, but you're not going to be, are you?" Not for them as a doctor. Not for her as…

"The only thing I'm doing to Lexington is providing a medical service. As far as anything else goes…" He shrugged. "I don't make plans much past tomorrow. Used to do that and I found out it doesn't pay off. So I don't do it any more. Which means that all I can tell you for sure is I'll be here tomorrow. Day after that…who the hell knows?"

Amazingly, she did understand that sentiment more than she wanted to. She hadn't made plans beyond the moment for a long, long time now either. But her reasons came from the accident, so what, in Cameron's life, had caused him to feel the same way? What deep conflict would cause someone who seemed like such a stable sort to develop that attitude toward life? Everybody had a buried hell, though, didn't they? Whatever his was, she supposed he had a good reason for a moment-to-moment life. She certainly did, as she'd seen close up how life could change, go from exciting to cruel with no warning, with all plans for the future damned. So why bother making them?

"You're correct about that," she said, shutting the closet door and heading back to the front of the clinic. "Making plans doesn't pay off. Better to go with the moment right now and let the next one take care of itself." Yet here she was, of all the stupid things she could do, making plans around something else that could be taken away from her in the blink of an eye. *Robby.*

Of course, Cameron was, too, whether or not he wanted to admit it. She wasn't about to point that out to him, though. It was easier letting him stay happy in his little delusion. For sure, she was happier staying in hers.

"Look, Danica, I've got to run over to Mr. O'Reilly and do his morning blood-sugar test then give him his insulin shot. It'll take me about twenty minutes give or take, depending on how much he wants to talk, then I'll be right back. Poke around, get rid of whatever you want, rearrange the furniture…" He grinned. "Play the piano. When I'm back we'll figure out what to do with this little boy of ours."

This little boy of ours. That had a very permanent ring to it for a man who shunned permanence. "He's not ours," she reminded him, trying to ignore the catch in her heart over those words.

"From the rumors I've been hearing this morning, he sure is ours. At least, according to half the town." For a while, anyway.

With that, Cameron ducked out the door, leaving Dani standing alone in his office with nothing to do except wait, as she didn't know how to play the piano—or the trombone. For the next fifteen minutes she pulled a few empty boxes from the storeroom and carried them to the curb for trash collection, wondering how the room was going to transform from clutter to playroom in the span of a very few hours. She pitched out old business records stashed in several boxes, some dating back fifty or sixty years, and boxes of discarded sheet music so yellowed and brittle it practically turned to powder. Then she actually stumbled across that rusty old trombone, propped in a corner behind an upturned table. On impulse, she carried it to Cameron's office, hiked herself up on his desk and was busy wedging it between the curtain rod and ceiling as a decoration of sorts when the front door jingled open.

"Doc!" someone yelled frantically from the front.

Dani scrambled down just as Greg LeMasters appeared in the doorway.

"Where's the doc?" He was out of breath, agitated, pacing back and forth in front of Cameron's door instead of stopping.

"He went to give Paddy O'Reilly his morning shot. He'll be back in a few minutes."

"I need help now! It's John Landers. He's having some kind of swelling thing going on." He raised his hands and indicated a swelled-up neck. "It's getting pretty big, and he's not looking so good. Kind of purple in the face. He said he got bit by a spider a little while ago, that it wasn't anything. But then about five minutes later he started to get dizzy. I've got him outside in the car, and I think it's bad, Dani. Real bad!"

"What kind of spider?" she asked, fearing the worst. In Indiana, the worst was a black widow or a fiddleback, either one meaning possible death. She held her breath for the answer, as she ran to the front door.

"Something little and yellow," he called after her.

She let out her breath. A yellow sac. Not lethal, unless someone was allergic to it. Which her gut reaction was telling her that Johan Landers was, and she trusted that first instinct. Her gut reaction was also telling her not to treat one of

Cameron's patients. But situations like this could go ugly very fast. She'd seen it happen. Treated people with horrible reactions from things other people had no reaction to at all. A yellow sac spider bite should sting like a bee, yet John was probably dying from it. That was a nudge of experience she couldn't ignore. Besides, by the time she made an initial assessment, Cameron would be back to take over. She hoped so anyway.

Once out on the sidewalk, Dani looked over at John, who'd slumped over in the front seat of the police car and was now gasping for breath. He was being strangled, and his neck was indeed swollen. She could see that even from a distance, and this was far worse than she'd expected. The man had mere minutes left, if even that long!

"I need a stethoscope," she ordered Greg. "Look in Cameron's office. And call someone to go find him." To save this man's life, she had to run back into the office for epinephrine, a drug that would reverse the reaction. She also had to find something to help sustain his breathing until it took effect. Yet she couldn't leave her patient alone to do all that!

Her patient. The thought of that made her queasy. Twice now in a few days she'd been forced into caring for a patient.

"See if Cameron's got some oxygen in there, too," she yelled out to Greg, as she ran to the driver's side door and crawled in. "John," she said as she squeezed in behind the steering-wheel. He responded with a nod, but he was frantic to breathe now, and she could hear audible gurgles coming from him…not so much from his chest as his throat. "Do you have an allergy?"

He tried to shake his head, at least his movement was what she interpreted as a no. "You don't carry a dose of epinephrine with you, do you?" Normally it came in a pen-like device that highly allergic people carried with them—people who could die from a bee sting or a food allergy. *Or spider bite.* In pen form, it made the lifesaving injection easy to deliver in an emergency such as this.

Again, John tried to indicate no, but it was apparent he was getting weaker by the second.

Frantically, Dani wedged herself down and over John and put an ear to his chest. She could hear air moving in and out, but not well, and not much. He was fighting for every breath and, like Greg had said, he was turning purple. "Look, I need to get you out of the car," she said, "and onto the sidewalk, so I can have a better look at you."

His neck was swollen even more than when she'd first seen him less than a minute ago, and now he was drooling, which indicated to her that his tongue might also be swelling. John was on the verge of dying here!

"Can you do that for me, John?" she asked, trying to keep her voice calm. "Can you help me help you get out of the car?"

He gave her a weak thumbs up, and she immediately climbed out of the car and ran back around to the passenger's side. "OK, now try and scoot yourself backwards. I've got you, so you won't fall, but I do need your help."

As he scooted, she pulled, and in seconds she had him out of the car and flat on the sidewalk. "I'm going to take a look," she said to him, as she began to run her fingers over his neck. She felt a little crackling under the skin and definite swelling. Immediately she opened his mouth to take a look, and what she saw…this man had mere seconds before he died if she didn't do something right now! His struggle to breathe was about to come to an end. His airway was swelling shut, his tongue was double in size, and there was almost no way now for air to get in. "Greg!" she screamed. "Have you found Cameron yet?"

Greg came running out the door with the stethoscope. "I put out the call. Someone's on the way to get him. What's wrong with John?" He mouthed, "Heart attack?"

Dani shook her head as she stuck the stethoscope in her ears to have a listen. She had to find a way to get air to his lungs right now or all the resuscitation in the world wouldn't bring him back. "Allergic reaction. Probably the spider." She stood up. "Watch him. I've got to go find some medicine." And something with which to do an emergency tracheotomy. "Do you know how to do mouth-to-mouth?"

He nodded, his face going ashen. "I've done it in training on the resuscitation dummy."

"Then do it on John if you need to. I'll be right back."

She turned to run into the office and bumped into Nina Owens coming down the sidewalk, her pregnant belly so round Dani almost didn't recognize her.

"What can I do?" Nina gasped.

"Trach set-up if he's got one, or anything that will suffice. Epi. Oxygen. IV set-up." Nina, the former office nurse, didn't bat an eye as she ran into Cameron's office for the supplies. Thank God she'd come along when she had, or it might have taken Dani too long to gather up what she would need to save John Landers's life. And there was no way Greg could be successful in mouth-to-mouth with someone whose airway had shut down. The resistance would be too great to get air in.

"I *need* Cameron," she told Greg again as she dropped back to her knees alongside John. "And call an ambulance."

She took a quick pulse on John. Weak, too fast. He was still conscious, fighting for breath but tiring quickly. "Stay with me, John," she said. "I know it's hard, but don't go to sleep. I need you to stay awake and keep fighting." The fear in his eyes... Dear God, she thought about Tom for an instant. *His windpipe had been crushed.* He'd suffered the way John was now, fighting for breath and losing the battle. Only he'd done it alone.

"Trach set-up," Nina said, running back to the sidewalk.

She was far too pregnant for this much activity. "And the epi. I'll go back for the rest."

"Be careful," Dani warned, jabbing John with the needle, hoping for an immediate reaction, which she knew wouldn't happen. His condition was too severe. The epi would keep him from getting worse and start the reverse action, but he needed respiratory support until then. Immediately, she grabbed up the sterile scrub for John's neck and poured it over him.

People were beginning to gather…all staying a respectful distance back. But watching and whispering. And they were all seeing the way her hands were shaking. She'd done a tracheotomy before. That wasn't what was making her nervous. The fact that she'd have to go in through all the swelling, which made the procedure more difficult, wasn't making her nervous either. She'd done this on humans, she'd done this on animals. No, it wasn't the procedure, it was just that… "No!" she said aloud. She had to get Tom out of her mind. *This was John. John Landers, not Tom McCain. Tom was dead, but she could save John!* "No," she whispered, willing the panic reaction away.

Taking a deep breath, bracing herself for what needed to be done, Dani tore open the surgical kit, spread the sterile drape out on the sidewalk and pulled on the gloves. It wasn't going to be a sterile procedure, but it was going to be as clean as she could keep it. "John," she said, realizing he was more unconscious than conscious now, and his breathing had faltered. "I've got to cut into your throat to your airway. Can you hear me?"

No response. And in that instant he did stop breathing.

In a flash, Dani grabbed up the paper package with the plastic trach tube and opened it, then opened the package with the scalpel in it. After that, she just did it. She went into emergency mode, like she had so many times before, and became a paramedic. In one swift cut she incised the skin, then she cut through the tissue and cartilage straight into the windpipe and waited for *that* sound…that one little whoosh when the patient caught a breath. And it came. Such a beautiful sound. A gurgle, a wheeze, then life.

To make sure the opening in his neck wouldn't shut, Dani stuck in the trach tube then smiled as his breaths started coming more easily. The epinephrine was already working and he was breathing. John would be fine shortly. A quick trip to the hospital and he might even be home later today.

It was amazing sometimes. Amazing…a miracle…the reason she'd become a veterinarian first, then a paramedic. Giving back a life, to man or beast, was a thrill she never got over.

As it became apparent to the crowd that John was going to live, they started applauding and cheering, and by the time Nina returned with an IV set-up, followed by Greg carrying a small oxygen cylinder, John was already beginning to pink up from getting air back into his lungs, and his eyes were beginning to flutter open.

Dani looked up at the crowd of twenty or so people, and saw Cameron pushing his way through. That's when she moved back to allow him room to work, slumped against the police car, and simply shut her eyes until it was over, until Cameron had stitched the trach tube into place, got the oxygen started, and put the IV in.

She was still sitting there when the ambulance came to take John to the hospital over in Everly and the crowd started to disperse. And when Cameron cleaned up the sidewalk from her impromptu little surgery. "Let's go inside now, Danica," he said gently, offering his hand to help her up. But she didn't take it. Didn't even open her eyes to see it.

"Danica?" He bent down to her. "It's over. John's going to be fine. You saved his life and he's already much better."

She still didn't open her eyes. Couldn't. She could hear him, but she wasn't ready yet. Wasn't ready to open her eyes and see what she knew she was finally going to see.

"Let's go into the office, Danica."

"I can't," she choked.

"You can't stay here on the street, sweetheart. We've got to get you inside."

"Can't."

Instead of trying to coax her any further, Cameron scooped Dani into his arms and carried her inside, straight to the first exam room. There he laid her on the table.

"Shock?" Nina asked.

Cameron shook his head as he stepped into the hall to join her. "More like full realization, I think."

"Look, Cameron, I'll come back tomorrow for my exam, if that's OK with you," Nina said. She'd been the first on his patient list for the morning.

"Are you OK?" he asked. "You were pretty busy there, too."

She patted her belly and smiled. "We're doing just fine. Tell Dani I'll come see her soon. Oh, and I'll post a notice on the door for your patients to call tomorrow and reschedule their appointments, then I'll lock the office on the way out so you two can be alone for a while. I think Dani needs that."

He thought the same thing, too, as he gave Nina's hand an affectionate squeeze then went back into the exam room with Dani. "Talk to me about it, Danica. Whatever it is, you've got to let it go now. You need to tell me what it is."

In her heart, she knew what Cameron said was right. But the words and the tears…once they started, she feared they would never stop.

It had been hours now, and she still wasn't talking. It was coming. He knew it. Recognized it. He'd done it himself almost three years, when he'd thought all he'd needed was a little holiday to help him get over feeling tired. It turned out he'd misdiagnosed himself. Or, more aptly, put off the obvious diagnosis. Rest, that's all he'd kept telling himself he needed. Overworked, overtired. Low-grade virus. Getting older. So many excuses, so he'd prescribed himself a holiday as a cure-all for all those afflictions. But one didn't get over leukemia simply by taking a holiday. He'd known that! Admitting had been another thing altogether, though!

"Physician, heal thyself," he said, pulling the skillet out of the cupboard and setting it on the stove burner. "Or kill thyself." As could have been the case, as he'd waited so long to submit himself to the tests. *Denial!* Of course, by that time the obvious could no longer be denied. Even the poorest excuse for a doctor couldn't have missed all the symptoms he'd been having, and he was a damned good doctor. For everyone but himself, anyway. Swollen gums, weight loss, low-grade fever, fatigue, headaches. He hadn't been kidding himself. Just trying to. *More denial!*

When he had finally given in and done what he should have done weeks sooner—taken the tests, got the results—it had nearly been a relief. Then he'd gone off to the beach and sat there for hours, merely staring at the water, trying not to think. In fact, he'd sat there all night and on through the next morning. Alone in the sand, listening to the waves—he had been sure that people walking by him had been wondering what was wrong with him…if he'd gone mad, or been on a bender and drunk himself into a stupor.

None of that had been the case. He'd merely been getting himself ready for what came next by, first, not thinking about his cancer, then by thinking about nothing except his cancer. One afternoon, one night, one morning, and he'd emerged in twenty-four hours ready to accept and deal with whatever was about to come at him. Much the same way Danica was doing now. So he did understand where she was. The reactions and emotions and feelings all clogged up in her would happen in her own good time, and he wasn't going to leave her, no matter how long that took.

Going through it alone was devastating. But going through it alone had been his choice. Oh, Sarah had wanted to be there, wanted to do the right thing by him, and he'd turned that into the first of so many times he'd pushed her away. In retrospect, he knew he'd been testing her. If she'd pushed back at him, she loved him. If she didn't… It wasn't fair to her, because she hadn't pushed back. She'd stayed, though. And in the black moments he'd accused her of doing it merely to save face. How bad would it look to walk out on a man with cancer? Yes, he'd used guilt to make her stay, and now, for the life of him, he couldn't understand why. She wasn't a bad woman. She just hadn't been up to his battles. Damn, he hated himself for all those months he'd wasted…Sarah's months. Months she couldn't get back. In the end, she'd been decent about it, while he'd been horrified by what he'd done.

And now here he was, taking care of someone who wanted to be alone. Except Danica wasn't pushing him away. And that did scare him. After her collapse, he'd brought her home from his office, put her to bed and tucked her under her favorite quilt, then made her tea and left her alone. For hours. Then a few minutes ago, she'd asked for something to eat. Which looked like it was going to be scrambled eggs and toast.

Someone who didn't know Danica might have said this was a breakdown in the making, and that she needed intervention in that direction. Something psychiatric. That wasn't right, though. She was merely getting ready. He knew the reaction, knew the start of it and how it would come out at the end. People dealt with their traumas in different ways. Some externalized their emotions, some delayed them. Some revved up right at the beginning and let it all out while some, like Danica, kept everything inside close to heart. But she would come through. She was too strong not to.

Until that time came, he would take care of her—bring her tea and food when she wanted it, leave her alone when that's what she needed.

Cameron turned his attention to grinding fresh pepper into the eggs he'd fixed, then he arranged them on a plate with the toast. It really wasn't like him to do this...to become so involved. He wasn't kidding himself, though. Had this happened at a different time in his life, it might have been more than one friend taking care of another. *Would* have been more, Danica willing. But now...well, scrambled eggs and toast was as far as he could commit. He hadn't come far enough for anything else. "Damn it to hell," he muttered, picking up the serving tray and heading up the back stairs to Danica's room. "Damn it *all* to hell."

CHAPTER EIGHT

THROUGH half-closed eyes, Dani watched Cameron stop in the doorway. He'd been here with her most of the day. Not fussing like he could have, for which she was grateful. Mostly he was allowing her the space she needed, and occasionally popping in to check on her, or bring her tea, and now whatever he had on the tray. She thought she'd smelled eggs cooking.

Earlier, she'd heard him on the phone, telling her grandmother and parents not to come, and she silently blessed him for that. She didn't want the fretting and tizzy over her condition they would bring. Or the worry and expressions of concern she would see on their faces. It wasn't fair to keep dragging them into her problems, and on a selfish level she wasn't ready to have anyone here, except Cameron.

In Cameron, there was none of that fussing or worry. In fact, what she saw in him was…understanding? It was like he knew exactly what she wanted or needed, and respected that. He kept his place, and allowed her hers, where her family had kept crowding her. They meant well, but crowding was crowding. And with Cameron, he seemed to know on some profoundly deep level exactly what was enough and what was too much. She didn't have to tell him, didn't have to ask him. It was just there, inside him.

He was an interesting man. Not at all like Tom. Tom's presence had filled every inch of space in the room. He walked in and instantly commanded attention, and people gave it to him like it was his due. But Cameron...his presence was as large, but in a very different way. He didn't have to command it. It just gravitated to him naturally. And it was reserved. Quiet and reserved. Someone at peace with who he was, she thought. Someone who had come to terms with himself and was at ease with what he'd found.

Tom hadn't gotten to that place. That's why he'd still taken so many risks. He hadn't achieved the level of self-awareness she saw in Cameron.

Cameron's self-awareness was nice, and she envied that. It was a place most people never found in themselves as they went through life, stepping from *terra firma* to quicksand then back onto *terra firma*. Like her life. But not Cameron. He was steady all the way. "Why do you always call me Danica?" she asked as he finally crossed through the room to her bedside.

"Dani is too personal." He sat the tray on the bedside stand and backed away. "I don't get too personal."

"But yet you've made me scrambled eggs. Isn't that personal?"

"There are different ways to achieve personal. To you, scrambled eggs might seem personal, but to me they seem more a basic element of concern. You need to eat, therefore I fixed you food."

"But without a personal relationship, you wouldn't feel the concern that would cause you to do that, would you? You don't scramble eggs for everyone you're concerned about. You were concerned about Nina's condition this morning, yet you didn't scramble her an egg."

"Your eggs are getting cold," he said, cocking an amused eyebrow at her. "I'd suggest you eat now and save debating them for later."

"You're a strange man, Cameron Enderlein," she said, picking up a piece of toast. "You know, I didn't like you that first day you walked by and called up to me. I didn't want to be bothered with you."

"And if I recall, you weren't. Didn't you simply sit there with your eyes closed and ignore me? For an entire week?"

"It was ten days." Dani took a bite of her toast, then washed it down with a little of her tea. "Every single morning, at precisely eight-fifteen."

"And yet you kept coming outside."

She smiled at him. "My porch, my right." She wasn't hungry, and she was eating only to be polite so she poked her way through the food, more pushing it from place to place on the plate than eating it, taking a few nibbles, until she simply didn't want to see it any more. Then he carried the tray away, and she was alone again.

Alone, and for the first time since the accident, she didn't want to be.

Sliding back under her quilt, she turned over on her side, her back to the door, and let the tears flow that had been threatening for hours now. Real tears, not the restrained tears she'd cried so many times before. Since John Landers's accident, all she'd seen in her mind had been Tom... The horrible images wouldn't go away. They were there, pounding at her. The way they'd parted, the way he'd died. She did have a visual image of that even though she hadn't seen any of it. Yet it was still so vivid, and it wouldn't let up, the same thing playing over and over...the school building collapsing, Tom trapped inside, Tom dying there alone. *Alone.*

Perhaps she didn't want the images to vanish. Not any more. She'd always known there would come a time to face them, and now...

Crying silently into her pillow, Dani extended her hand

across to the bedside stand for a tissue, but as she reached out, Cameron tucked it into her hand. Then, without a word, he stretched out on the bed next to her and pulled her into his arms, then let her cry as she hadn't cried before. There were no words between them, no need for them. Her heart was breaking and he knew that. Words would have only gotten in the way, so he held her and rocked her and stroked her hair, giving her the gentle support she so terribly needed. He didn't back away from the tears, didn't care that she was soaking the front of his shirt, didn't care that it didn't end quickly and neatly. For an hour, as the tears subsided, then gushed again, sometimes in such hard, racking sobs her entire body shook, sometimes in a quiet flow where she barely breathed, Cameron held onto her, and told her things no one had ever said before…things that didn't come in words, but came from his heart to hers. Then, when she was cried out, and nothing was left but dry, heavy sobs, he brought her a cold, damp washcloth for her face.

"I'll bet I look terrible," she said, her voice still hiccupping with the last of her tears.

"I've seen worse," he said gently. "And you don't look so bad with a red nose. It's kind of cute with your fair complexion. Gives you a nice look of distinction."

She looked up at him, trying to smile. "I'm so sorry, Cameron. I didn't mean to do this, to involve you."

He stretched out on the bed with her again and pulled her back into his arms. "There's nothing to be sorry about, Danica. Nothing at all."

"But there is so much," she whispered, realizing the time had finally come. After all these months, with the unthinkable half-thoughts pounding at her, and trying to ignore them, she was finally brave enough to do this now. Brave enough, only because of Cameron. *And only with Cameron.* "It was my fault he died. My fault Tom was killed." And there it was. Everything she'd been pushing away for so long. Now she was admitting it to Cameron, telling him the deep, ugly truth about that day. And it was like he was the one who was supposed to hear it. She didn't understand why, didn't even want to think about it. But it felt as if she'd been on hold, waiting for this moment for such a long time. "I was the senior medic when we went out on that call. We'd heard there was a possibility of a collapsed school so we took a few volunteers along. When we got there, the building was only partially down and we needed an assessment before anybody was to go in. I knew better than to let Tom go off on his own like he did. We never searched a scene alone. *Never.* Gideon's rules."

"Gideon?"

"Gideon Merrill. One of the doctors in charge of Global Response. He always stressed that the rules were for our benefit—to keep us as safe as possible in a difficult situation. He said it wasn't always easy to follow the rules, but it was mandatory, and I've seen him go so far as to pull someone off a rescue if they broke the rules. I knew that, Cameron. I knew what could happen, and yet I—"

"Didn't Tom know that, too?" he interrupted.

Her head to his chest, she nodded, then sniffled. "But he was different. Everybody knew that, including Gideon. Tom always did things in a different way…in his own way, kind of the way Gideon did, and Gideon never follows his own rules. And Tom…he always took the bigger risks, always pushed the rules to the edge. He was the guy who did the most dangerous rescues, the one who went into places no one else could, or would. It was like he looked for the adventure, but not really, because none of it was for himself, or for the thrill of doing something on the edge. Some people are that way, you know. They live on the edge because they like the adrenalin rush that goes with it. But I think Tom's rush came from knowing he could accomplish things no one else could, from saving people who might not otherwise be saved. He thrived on that. Looked for the opportunities. And we all accepted that in him."

Dani paused, taking in a deep breath. She was relaxing a little now, not feeling like she was so close to the edge of the cliff and ready to fall off, like she had been a while ago. It was so easy talking to Cameron, saying things to him she'd never said to anyone else. Admittedly, she liked being here in his arms, too. It was safe, but it was also nice, and not in the way that it was nice because he was protecting her and she liked the feel of being protected. It was different somehow. She couldn't define what that was, but there were certainly some strong feelings going on she'd never felt before. Feelings like…like she was where she belonged.

OK, so now she was being silly! This was just proximity. Cameron was here, he was steady, and she needed somebody steady to be with her. That's all it could be. At least, that's what she wanted to believe.

"So how was it your fault if Tom knowingly took the bigger risks? The decisions were his and apparently the leader of your group accepted that as part of the operation. You, yourself, said you were obliged to follow Gideon's rules, yet Gideon allowed Tom to break them without consequences. So it can't be your fault that he did, because those choices were made without including you in them."

"They were, and I understand that, but I should have told him no. Should have…" She choked. Somehow, she should have stopped him. "I didn't try hard enough, and he died because of it, Cameron. He died because I didn't do my job and stop him. I just let him go." Funny, she'd expected another wash of tears when she finally said the awful words, yet surprisingly they didn't come. "It was my responsibility to keep him safe, to keep anybody safe who went out with me and make sure they did what they were supposed to do…make sure Tom did what he was supposed to do. But I didn't do my job." Still, no tears.

"Exactly what would Tom have done if you'd demanded he not go? Would he have listened to you and stayed behind? Would he have argued? Would he have totally ignored you, Danica? Turned his back on you and walked away, knowing you didn't want him to go?"

Such harsh words. "That's not fair," she protested. "You didn't know him."

"I think what you've told me is enough for me to draw my own conclusions. So, am I right, Danica?" He whispered the last words, not seductively but almost like he didn't want her to hear them, or didn't want to hurt her with them. And they did hurt, because he was right. She might have tried harder to stop Tom, but he wouldn't have listened to her.

Dani didn't answer right away. Instead, an image of that day flashed through her mind as she drew in a deep breath and held it. The school…the collapsed ceiling. There had been no sure way in, and Dag had been acting like there was a survivor inside. She'd known Dag was never wrong, so had Tom. "We need back-up," she whispered, as if she were back there, reliving everything that had happened. "I'm calling Gideon, Tom. He'll send us more volunteers so we can get the building secured. It won't take long!"

"If there's someone in there, we can't wait, Dani," Tom had argued. "You know I can't wait." Can't wait…can't wait…

"We've got to get help first!"

Yet he had gone in. *But she had tried to stop him.*

Even now she could see him running to the back of the structure, his long legs carrying him through the mud and debris like he was running a sprint on a race track. "No," she whispered, as he tossed her a dismissive wave over his shoulder—the one he always did, the one that told her he was going to do what he had to do, that he'd be fine. Then he was gone. That was it. He'd made his choice. "Tom, don't do it…" she whispered. Then her eyes blinked wide, and she went rigid against Cameron's chest. "Tom, I'm ordering you. Don't go in there!"

A stray tear trickled down her cheek. "I couldn't stop him, Cameron. I remember it now. I told him not to go…*ordered him not to go*…and he wouldn't stop for me."

"It wasn't just you, Danica. He wouldn't have stopped for anybody. Probably not even for Gideon. That's the way some people are, and we can't change them."

Dani went limp in Cameron's arms again. "He died of a crushed windpipe, and today, with John…"

"Oh, my God, Danica. I didn't know that. I'm so sorry." He pulled her even closer. "I'm so sorry," he whispered, stroking her hair.

"If Tom had loved me enough, he wouldn't have gone in. He wouldn't have…"

"No, sweetheart, don't do that to yourself. Don't blame yourself for what Tom did, or second-guess his love for you, because one has nothing to do with the other. I didn't know him, but I'm sure he was the kind of person who acted because he had to. Going in like he did, disobeying the rules, was simply part of his make-up, and it wasn't about his feelings for you. He didn't disrespect you or even disregard you. He merely acted true to himself, and that's such a big difference. And in the end, being true to yourself is the greatest strength any person can have."

"But I've thought that if I'd just loved him enough, then he would have loved me enough to listen. Maybe he knew that I didn't have all the feelings for him I should have." Dear God, these were the words she'd never wanted to say, the feelings she'd never wanted to admit. They were so deep, and so ugly. But she'd had doubts. Not about Tom, but about what Tom had to be, and what she couldn't be for him.

"It's not about how much you loved him, sweetheart. Or how much he loved you. It's about who he was. Tom was bound to do what he had to do no matter how much you tried to stop him, and I think, deep down, you do know that. He was true to himself, even though he knew what it might cost him, and for that, he was a man to be admired."

"A hero," she whispered.

"Was there a survivor in the accident?" he asked.

"A little girl. She's fine. Back safe and sound with her family."

"That's the way he would have wanted it to turn out. I think you were lucky to have him in your life, Danica, and there's nothing to doubt. Not if your feelings were deep enough, not if you could have changed the outcome. Leave it there, as a cherished memory, and don't hang onto the rest of the doubts. Just remember that you had a special man in your life, one who loved you and one whom you loved."

Two very special men. And neither of them destined to stay in her life for very long.

A feeling of contentment mixed with a bit of melancholy washed over her and she snuggled even more into Cameron's embrace. She wanted to stay there for a while, not because she needed to be comforted but because she needed to be with Cameron.

"Nobody?" Dani asked, pacing back and forth on her front porch.

"Just the grandmother," Cameron said, referring to Robby's grandmother. "And according to the director of the nursing care facility she's in, she doesn't even know she has a grandson."

"So he's yours." They were expecting the hospital social worker to deliver Robby any minute now.

Dani smiled as she alternately paced then looked out toward the road. She hadn't had any practical experience with toddlers, but she knew Cameron would be having a sudden awakening very shortly. At such a young age, Robby would adapt quickly, and the nice, docile, recovering little child Cameron was hoping for would turn into a rambunctious little boy with his own ways.

Dani was excited to see what they were, actually. She knew Robby was bright. She'd seen that in his sad eyes.

"He's not mine," Cameron protested. "I don't want a child, and I'm doing this only because he deserves better than what he was about to get. No child deserves the guardian home."

So he said, but she did notice he was pacing as much as she was. Perhaps he wasn't going to admit how much he wanted Robby, but she could see it on his face. It did concern her, though, what would happen when a permanent home for Robby was found—and that *would* happen. Sooner or later Robby would be put into the permanent custody of a long-lost relative or an adoptive family. Either way, how would Cameron take that? He wanted to act all big and blustery, like having the child here with him didn't really matter, but she knew better. For Cameron, it did matter. He'd gone out of his way to make it matter.

It mattered for her, too. And as she watched Cameron stretch to look down the road for a sign of the social worker's car, she actually wondered if Cameron might consider adopting Robby himself. That way, she wouldn't have to lose the boy either. Or, perhaps, the father?

She shook her head, trying to get rid of that cozy image. Where had it come from anyway? This wasn't about a relationship between Cameron and her. Not in any form. It was about doing what was best for a child who'd just lost his mother in a tragic accident. That's all. "What if other arrangements for him can't be made quickly?"

"Get through the moment and let the next one take care of itself," he reminded her as the car finally came into view.

"So you wouldn't ever consider keeping him?" OK, so maybe

this wasn't exactly the best thing to ask him at a time like this. Especially as the look her gave her was a rather surly scowl.

"What I'm considering right now is what he'd like to have for lunch, as it's almost that time. Beyond that, I'll think about dinner, then bedtime and nothing else."

He did avoid all things permanent, didn't he? All things permanent, all things in his future. What other things did Cameron avoid? she wondered, as he trotted down the front walk to meet the car coming to a stop in front of the house.

The exchange took about twenty minutes, and all through it Dani stood back and watched. Cameron got his instructions from the social worker, a very tired-looking woman who seemed only too glad to be handing Robby to a complete stranger. She gave Cameron a little bag of clothes and toys, she had him sign papers, then she was gone, and Cameron was literally standing at the curb, clutching a small boy in his arms. Cameron, with a worried look on his face that almost made him look like a small boy, too.

The two of them, Dani thought as she motioned them up to the porch. They definitely needed each other. Robby already knew that. It was evident in the way he clung to Cameron. And soon Cameron would know that, too. "I have cheese sandwiches ready," she called to them.

Cameron merely stood there, not budging, not blinking. She wasn't even sure if he was breathing.

"Are you two coming?"

"What have I done, Danica?"

She laughed. "Taken a little bit of permanence into your life, I'd say." And hers, too, she hoped. For now, anyway.

"It's not medical," Dani assured Cameron as he did a cursory exam of Robby for the third time that afternoon. Lunch had been a disaster. Food on the floor, food on the walls, milk in

Cameron's lap. Then the bathroom accident. Cameron was convinced Robby wasn't feeling well but she was convinced the boy was protesting about his situation. Nothing in his world had been the way it was supposed to be these past few days and under the circumstances she thought Robby was actually behaving very well. But poor Cameron was a wreck. "He's just frightened. Once he's more sure of us, and used to the way we do things, he'll calm down."

"Why is it that women get the natural instincts when it comes to children and men have to *learn* how to take care of them?"

Dani laughed. "Oh, I think your instincts are there. I just don't think you're conditioned to use them."

"Well, I hope you're right and mine surface pretty damned fast because I don't know what I'm going to do."

"Run to the store for some diapers," she suggested.

"But he's toilet trained."

She glanced over at Robby, who was sitting on the floor in the kitchen corner, glaring at both of them like he wanted to kill them. His little face was scrunched up into anger and hatred, but through it all his eyelids were drooping over beautiful blue eyes. He wanted to sleep but he was fighting it. Shortly, he would lose the battle and they could tuck him into bed for a while. Without his mother. Every time Dani thought about that, tears welled up in her eyes. Right now, if the choice were hers, she would have held Robby, pulled him into her arms to comfort him. But he wanted to be left alone, and she did understand that. Better than most people would. Going through a tragedy, there were times to be left alone and times to be surrounded by people who cared. Understanding that didn't quell her desire to comfort him because, for the first time since she'd learned she couldn't bear children, new hope was dawning. Someone did have to give Robby a real home after all. Why not her? Why sit around keeping her fingers crossed that Cameron would keep him, which would allow her to stay near Robby? Cameron wasn't going to be permanent here, but she was, and she could be Robby's mother. She already loved him. Love at first sight.

Crazy idea? She wasn't sure. Perhaps it was, or perhaps it was brilliant.

Time to think, she decided. She needed time to think about it. Yet when she looked over at Robby sitting in the corner, trying to glare so defiantly at her through sleepy eyes, just daring her to bother him, she was pretty sure she'd done all the thinking she needed to. God willing, this had to be her child. For Linda, for Robby. And for her.

But for Cameron, too?

"He may have been toilet trained, but I have a feeling we need to expect a little regression in some of his behavior for a while."

"Diapers," Cameron muttered on his way to the door.

"Big ones. Toddler size." She smiled, arching her eyebrows playfully. "And a bottle of wine. Something tells me you're going to need it for yourself before the night's over." Dani glanced over at Robby again, and saw that he'd finally nodded off to sleep. Instead of disturbing him by picking him up and carrying him to a bedroom upstairs, when Cameron had gone, Dani tucked a blanket over Robby and left him where he was on the floor, then slid down next to him. "Beautiful boy," she whispered, brushing a lock of blond hair from his eyes, then brushing a tear from her own. "You're going to be fine. I promise, you're going to be fine." Then she took his tiny hand in hers and simply watched him as he slept.

"I can't do this," Cameron whispered to himself, as he finally sat down in his easy chair, kicked off his shoes, and let out a breath of relief. There'd been lunch, then dinner. Robby had refused to eat more than a few bites either time. He'd intermittently cried, slept and thrown temper tantrums. Oh, and the bathroom accidents. Three of them, all because he refused to wear the diapers. "It's crazy. I was out of my mind."

Danica had been such a help all day, and he'd hoped she'd volunteer on into the night, but she hadn't. After a futile dinner of chicken and mashed potatoes carried in from the diner, she'd shooed them out the door to go home while she cleaned up the mess. And she'd laughed at him for fretting over spending the night alone with Robby.

"What the hell was I thinking, agreeing to do this?"

He hadn't been thinking. That's what! Of all the people in the world to look after a child, he wasn't the one to do it. Hell, he wasn't even doing a good job of taking care of himself, so what gave him the right to bring somebody else into his life? Because Robby deserved better than the institution, that's what gave him the right. He was a lost child, and Cameron knew what that felt like. Peanut-butter allergy and earaches aside, Robby needed someone who understood, and Cameron understood. Danica understood, too.

And the way she looked at Robby in unguarded moments… "I hope this isn't a mistake," he whispered, reaching to the table next to his recliner for a glass of wine. She already loved the boy, no denying that. That worried him, because Danica didn't deserve more heartbreak. But heartbreak was inevitable when a permanent home was found for Robby. Unless… "Dumb plan," he muttered, trying to block it out of his head. Danica and Robby? And him?

Really dumb plan. Danica and Robby together, perhaps. But he wasn't part of that equation. Couldn't be, especially if the boy was to be involved. So what was he doing, dreaming of this cozy little family he had no right to be part of? For him, taking care of Robby temporarily was nothing more than a little streak of compassion coming to the surface, forcing him to do things he knew he shouldn't, things to which he had no right yet. It was that look—the one in Robby's eyes. He saw that look in the mirror when he wasn't careful. And saw it in Danica's eyes, too. Three people who had all known losses in their lives. Such a kinship.

Yet, as much as he wanted to, he still couldn't include himself in it.

Dani glanced at the red light on the digital alarm clock next to her bed, trying to wake herself up. Just after midnight. The noise…phone ringing. It took a second for that to sink in, then when it did she grabbed up the handset. "Hello, Cameron," she said immediately.

"How did you know?"

"You've called three times this evening. Why wouldn't it be you this time?" A tiny smile creased her face. Was she sure a night-time diaper would be good for Robby as he wasn't a baby? That had been the first call. The second had been about a nightlight. The third about…well, she wasn't sure about that one. It had had something to do with a before-bedtime drink of water versus milk, then on to how to brush Robby's teeth and did it matter that Robby kept pulling off his pajama bottoms?

"He's crying. Has been for an hour. He wants his mommy."

Poor Robby, she thought. Poor Cameron. "He'll cry himself to sleep eventually." Like she really knew. But it seemed logical. Some kind of motherly instinct going on in her, she supposed. That, and the fact that puppies did the same thing. Only her remedy for that was to wrap a ticking clock in a towel and stick it in the bed with the pup, and eventually it would cuddle up with the clock and think the ticking was its mother's heartbeat. All children needed to feel that heartbeat, she thought, whether they were humans or puppies. "He'll exhaust himself, then go to sleep."

"And in the meantime?"

"Love him, Cameron. Hold him tight, let him know that

someone's taking care of him tonight. He's frightened. He needs that." Just as she'd needed it only yesterday. And Cameron was so good at it. It would be a tough first night for both these men in her life, but they would come through.

"And what if I go to sleep and...squeeze him or smother him or drop him?"

Well, perhaps one of the men in her life would come through. The other, it seemed, would fret himself into a nervous break-down. "You're a doctor, what do you advise your new mothers?"

"I advise my new mothers to find a pediatrician, which I am not. And it's showing."

She laughed. "So what do you want me to do, Cameron?"

"Tell me there's a lullaby that will always do the trick."

"Want to come spend the night with me? Maybe between the two of us we can get him settled down."

"Never has a man wanted to hear those words more than I do," he said, already feeling optimistic about the outcome of this first night with Robby. Of course, he would have preferred hearing those words in a completely different context. Last night, as he'd stretched out on her couch, he'd come so close to going up the stairs. He'd wanted to. The urge had certainly been there in ways he'd never expected. Would he have tried it, though?

No. He would not have. Simple as that.

But thinking about it had been nice as he'd drifted off to sleep. "Fifteen minutes. Give me time to get Robby into the car, and we'll be right there." And Robby would be the one to sleep with Danica tonight while he, again, stayed downstairs. He was sure of that. Lucky boy.

"Robby!"

The instant she said his name, Robby wiggled out of Cameron's arms and flew straight into Dani's. She was bending down, arms wide open to greet him, and he hit her with such force he knocked her backwards. Cameron was immediately at her side.

"Are you OK?" he asked, trying to pull Robby off her. But Robby wouldn't be pulled, and he held onto her for all he was worth, his tiny hands wrapped around her neck, his head pressed to her chest.

"Fine." She laughed, holding onto Robby almost as tightly as he was holding onto her. "I've been knocked down under a lot of circumstances, by big dogs and trees and collapsing roofs, but never by a three-year-old." She did manage to push him away from her a little bit. "I think we should get up off the floor," she told him. "Will you let Dr....?" She paused, frowning up at Cameron. "What have you told him to call you?"

Cameron shrugged. "Nothing."

"He does talk, you know." She got to her knees, then stood and picked Robby up off the floor and held him, propped on her left hip. "So, Robby. This is Dr. Cameron Enderlein. Can you say that?"

Robby's response was to bury his head into Dani's shoulder.

"I didn't think so. So, why don't you just call him D—"

"Not the D-word," Cameron said in a panic.

"D, as in?"

"Daddy," he said.

She smiled. "I was going to say Doc. I think Robby will be able to handle that. Don't you think so, Robby?" she asked the boy. "Can you say Doc?"

"Hungry," Robby replied.

"Well, I should say so. You haven't eaten anything all day, have you?"

His head still tucked into her, he shook it.

"Then I say we have some cookies and milk before you go off to bed."

"Not nutritionally sound," Cameron warned.

"And you would suggest what?"

He thought about it for a moment, then relented. "Cookies and milk."

"And you're invited to come, too." With that, she spun around and headed to the kitchen, with Robby bobbing up and down on her hip. It was a good feeling, actually. Gave her something to think about for her future. That little glimmer of hope continued.

"How'd you do that?" Cameron asked from the hallway outside Dani's bedroom door. "He's been down two minutes, and he's fast asleep."

"He's exhausted. Like I told you earlier, it was bound to happen." She pulled the door shut, then slumped against the wall, too tired to figure out what to do next. Crawl into bed with Robby? Sleep on the chaise next to the bed? Go downstairs to keep Cameron company?

"You're exhausted, too, aren't you?" he asked sympathetically.

"No more than you are, but it's a good exhaustion. I like doing something worthwhile again."

"I was out of line that day." He moved in closer. So close, in fact, she could smell the faint trace of aftershave lotion lingering on him. Musk. She did like that on him. Liked the masculinity, and the familiarity. She didn't think she could ever grow tired of it.

"No, you weren't. You were right. The words stung a little bit, but the truth does that sometimes, doesn't it?" Funny how the only thing she wanted right now was to melt into his arms. No, she didn't need comfort like she had last night. She merely craved the feel of him. It had been so nice at a time when it had been desperately needed, and now she wanted to try it because... Actually, she didn't know why. She just wanted to. Of course, that was the exhaustion talking. Dangerous talk, for if he'd offered, she would have accepted. *Eagerly.* But he was standing at a respectable distance from her. Safe, and somewhat stiff, actually. She saw that in him so often. One minute he was relaxed and friendly, being a casual friend and maybe even inching his way into more, then the next minute he would stiffen up like he'd caught himself at something he shouldn't do. Just like now.

Did she want more with Cameron? If someone were to ask her that question on the spur of the moment, her immediate reaction would be an adamant no! But if she were to have a little think on it... Well, perhaps it was for the best that he kept his distance because she wasn't sure what she would say with all the crazy, mixed-up things going on inside her. And that scared her in ways she didn't want to be scared.

It intrigued her, too. Which scared her even more.

CHAPTER NINE

WHEN Dani shoved open the bakery door, a gust of wind swirled in with her and blew a stack of paper napkins off the display counter. The half-dozen tables Nora had set up in a small café-style area were filled with people all munching various forms of pastries, drinking exotic coffee concoctions and speculating about the weather. It was a blustery day—not cold, but windy. There were storms on the way and shortly after Cameron had left for work that morning, she'd decided she and Robby would go to his office and wait out the storms there with him, which would give her a chance to talk to Cameron about what she'd had on her mind all night and all morning. She wanted to adopt Robby and now it was time to see what Cameron had to say about it. Even see if he had any notions of adopting Robby himself.

"So that's him?" Nora asked, running out from behind the counter, first to give Dani a hug then to bend down and give one to Robby. As she stretched out her arms to him, he immediately stiffened and backed away, hiding himself protectively behind Dani's legs.

"Go away!" he huffed, his face contorted in anger, peeking out at Nora.

"He doesn't handle personal attention very well yet," Dani

explained. "He wants his M-A-M-A." She spelled the word. "And he's very angry that she's not coming for him."

"Poor thing, can you blame him?"

Dani shook her head. No, she couldn't blame him. She only prayed that she could get through to him on some level. And that he wouldn't be whisked away to yet another strange place with strange people before she had a chance to see about the steps necessary to keep him with her. "I thought you might have something to take his mind off his situation."

"As a matter of fact, I have a fresh batch of sugar cakes just out of the oven. They're shaped like bunnies, with lots of pink sugar sprinkled on top." With that, Nora bustled off to get a cake while Dani glanced over at the window as several people stood to get a better look outside. The wind had died down a bit, she noticed. But what she noticed more than that was an odd hue to the sky. It had just gone green. Immediately, the warning hairs stood up on the back of her neck. She was afraid she knew the dire implications blowing in with this storm. "Nora, have you got a radio here?" she yelled.

"In the storage room in the rear."

Without waiting, Dani scooped Robby into her arms and ran to the back room, where she tuned the radio in to the weather station. Severe thunderstorms were what they were predicting. Heavy rain, hard winds, but no mention of a tornado. She was too experienced to believe what she was hearing, though. These things didn't always get predicted. Typical tornadoes as well as deadly straight lines…sometimes they escaped the radar and this, she feared, was one of those times. The prickling hairs on the back of her neck and the cold chills shooting up her spine told her not to discount her feelings with this one. She'd see the disastrous results of unpredicted weather to

"Nora, do you have a basement here?"
the woman. "Or a storm cella

"Why?" Nora asked, her face blanching. "What's going on?"

"I think it's a tornado," Dani whispered. "The weatherman says it's a thunderstorm coming in, but he's not saying anything about a tornado and I think that's what's coming. We've got to take cover. Now! Because I don't think we've got much time."

Nora pointed to the door leading downstairs, and Dani thrust Robby into her arms. "Take him down there and make sure he's safe." She gave Robby a kiss on the cheek, and felt a catch in her throat. She didn't want to leave him behind, but she couldn't take him with her. It wasn't safe and Robby had to be safe! Nora would see to that, but Dani desperately wanted it to be her taking care of Robby, and she was torn between duty and the boy she wanted for a son.

"He'll be fine with me," Nora reassured her, seeing the look of despair on Dani's face. "I promise you, Dani, I'll take care of him like he's my own."

"I know, but it's so hard…" She gave Robby another quick kiss then stepped away.

"Mama!" he screamed, reaching out his arms to her.

Dear God, this hurt. "I'm sorry," she whispered to him.

"Mama!" he screamed again. This time Nora turned him away from Dani so Robby couldn't see her and she couldn't see Robby.

"You've got to go," Nora said. "It's what you do, Dani. You've got to go warn people, and I'll take care of your little boy."

It was what she did. Swallowing back a hard, bitter lump in her throat, Dani ran to the front of the shop. "Tornado!" she shouted. "Everybody get down into Nora's basement! Right now!"

The dozen or so people there dropped their coffee-mugs on the tabletops and pastries on the floor, smashing them underfoot as they ran to take shelter. But Dani didn't follow them. She watched out the window for several moments after ⌐had gone to the basement, then opened the door to ⌐⌐⌐weatherman was reporting this wrong, chances were many of the people here didn't know yet. *Cameron probably didn't know.*

She stepped out onto the sidewalk and felt the sudden chill of the dropping temperature. It happened before thunderstorms and tornadoes, that last-minute plunge in temperature coming with the quick dip in barometric pressure. It caused her to shiver, and instinctively, she huddled into herself as she started to scurry along the sidewalk. Then suddenly everything around her went still. Deathly still. The birds quit singing, the whistling of the wind went totally quiet. The feeling was surreal, like the storm had vanished into a sea of nothing. Then all of a sudden, in the distance… Not daring to breathe, Dani listened to the sound now coming into range. "Oh, my God," she whispered when the realization hit her. It was *the* sound. *The freight train.* People always said a tornado coming in sounded like a freight train, and they were right. It did.

It was on its way, not too far off now, and all she could think about was Cameron.

Dani looked up into the sky, then turned and ran as fast as her legs would carry her down the street to Cameron's office, stopping at each little shop along the way long enough to open the door and scream, "Tornado's coming!" then rush on to the next door.

By the time she was halfway down the block, the wind was beginning to churn again, this time carrying with it bits of debris from the street—leaves and sticks. Sand blowing up from the river shore blew into her eyes, its grit stinging them to tears. She knew better than to rub at them, because that could cause a corneal abrasion—a scratch. So she blinked frantically, hoping the tears would do the cleansing, and continued on, weaving in and out of people on the street who were now aware of what was happening and running for their own lives, trying to find cover in the various buildings along the way. Even the people in cars stopped, got out and ran into shops. Better to not be in a car, according to experts. Lie low in a ditch, take cover in a basement, get out of the car, stay away from the windows.

As she scanned the mental checklist, the impulse to turn around and look for the tornado overtook her, and she did so. All she saw was the sky turning a darker, angrier green. All she heard was the freight train getting closer. It was going to plow through any time, stopping for nothing and no one.

Dani turned back and kept running to Cameron's office. When she reached it, the wind was hitting so hard she was nearly panting. "Tornado," she screamed as she yanked open the door. A wind gust ripped it right from her hands, tore it off the hinges, and by the time Dani turned around to have a look, it was blowing down the middle of the street, end over end.

"Cameron!"

"Dani?" he said, rushing out of the storage room. "What's wrong?"

"Tornado," she gasped, still running for the back. "Does this building have a basement?"

He shook his head.

Above them, the roar of the wind was getting louder. Too loud! "Get down," she choked, running directly at Cameron and knocking him backwards on the floor as the front plate-glass window exploded and a cement flowerpot that had decorated the curbside came through, spraying glass and daffodils everywhere. It hit the wall next to where they were lying on the floor then dropped in a loud thunk mere inches away.

"Dani," Cameron said, pushing her off him then rolling over, jumping up and pulling her along with him. "In the bathroom. It's an interior wall."

Interior rooms were said to be safer because if they came down they didn't bear the weight of an outside wall with all its supports to hold up the building.

Cameron pushed Dani ahead of him and when they got in,

he closed the door. Not that it would do any good. Then this time he was the one to knock her to the floor.

It was a small room, not really big enough for the two of them to stretch out, so they piled on top of each other, faces to the floor, Cameron literally sprawled over Dani's back, and wedged themselves between the toilet and the wall. "Where's Robby?" he shouted above the noise.

"Nora Carston's basement. The safest place I could think of." Maybe it was safe, but she desperately wanted Robby safe in her arms right now as much as she wanted to be safe in Cameron's arms. The three of them safe together—her only wish.

Outside the bathroom, more glass was shattering. And it sounded like things were being picked up and thrown back down. Large things. The reception desk. The piano. It was an indescribable sound. She'd survived hurricanes and mudslides. She'd traipsed the perimeter of a forest fire and watched an avalanche. But never had she heard anything like this. Or felt anything like it, the way the pressure was beginning to build up. Her ears were popping, it felt like her eardrums were expanding and contracting, on the verge of exploding.

The roar of a real freight train seemed benign compared to all this. Outside this tiny area of security, walls were coming down and objects she couldn't identify were blowing through the last of the existing walls. And as the world was seeming to come to an end around them, Cameron moved to cover even more of her, to literally put his life over hers and take care of her. Cameron, the man she depended on. The man with whom she was falling in love. What a bad time for that full realization to hit, but maybe it was because of that time. If she didn't survive, and there was a chance they might not, knowing that she loved Cameron Enderlein was something nice to have at the end.

"What should we do?" he shouted almost directly into her ear. "You're the emergency expert here. What should we do?"

"Stay together," she shouted back. Stay close to Cameron. Pray for Robby.

"In case we don't make it," he shouted over the continual roar, "there's something I think you should know."

Admissions at the deathbed. She'd heard them before. People wanting to confess or profess something with their last breath. If he did that, she feared it would seal their fate and she didn't want it sealed, not here, not like this. "No!" she screamed. Tom had said something like that on their way up the mountain that day. *In case we don't make it out of here...* But it had been in jest. He'd willed her his stethoscope, his bicycle and a basket full of dirty laundry back home. All meant in fun, of course. But then he'd died. And now she couldn't hear another *in case we don't make it out of here.* "Whatever you want to tell me, I don't want to hear it!"

Dani raised up a little to repeat herself, and as she did so a loud shrieking cracking noise overhead caused Cameron to push flat down on her. In that split second, the ceiling collapsed. Large chunks of plaster dropped to the floor as the roof lifted up and went flying into the sky. Then the sink base just a meter away from them was sucked out along with it, as was the supply cabinet right next to it. And the toilet directly next to them!

There was no time to think about options, no time to brace for anything because the first interior wall came down on them. Through it all, water from the broken toilet and sink pipes spewed up into the air like an artesian well springing up in the wrong place. "I love you," Dani whispered. Not a confession, not even a profession. Merely something to comfort her as another wall came crashing down nearby.

She couldn't feel Cameron with her now. Physically she couldn't discern his weight on top of her, and deep inside she didn't feel the little tingle he caused. Even though there was nothing to confirm what she was feeling, she knew Cameron was no longer there with her, and she didn't want to move for fear of what she'd find…or wouldn't find. Didn't want to look, didn't want to breathe. And so she stayed there for the next minute, praying, begging, bargaining with God as huge trees ripped up by the roots went flying overhead, and road signs and furniture and other random parts of people's lives went sailing off into oblivion.

Then, as quickly as it had come, it went. Three minutes that had seemed like an eternity, and it was over. And she was blessedly alive. Under a pile of rubbish, but alive.

Her first thought was for the poor people in the next place that would face the same fury, and her second thought was for Cameron. "Cameron!" she shouted, trying to inch her way around under the pile of building debris on top of her. It wasn't so heavy as to weigh her down, but she still had to be careful. There was no telling what was mixed in the debris—glass, nails, kitchen knives—practically anything, and most of it with the potential to hurt her. But she'd survived, and she wasn't going to let herself get hurt. Not this time. "Cameron, can you hear me?"

Cautiously, Dani wiggled out from under a large chunk of plaster, then pushed aside several of the wooden stud boards from the wall. She managed to poke a hole through all the debris but there was too much dust to see anything yet. She could feel the dry grit of it creeping down into her lungs. "Cameron, if you can hear me, let me know. Give me a sign."

How could he have gotten off her? Why would he have gotten off her? Unless… She choked back a sudden sob. Had the tornado sucked him up? It happened. People disappeared in these things. "Cameron!" she screamed. Overcome by panic to find him, followed by an adrenalin rush, she pushed her way though the rest of the debris on top of her, safety risks be damned. If he was here, she had to get to him! "Where are you? Can you hear me?" Dear God, if she found him and he'd survived this…

"Out here!" Cameron shouted. It was muffled.

"Cameron?" Finally, she turned fully over, and what she saw… No part of the building remained standing. Not one wall. It was like a wrecking ball had come through and knocked it completely to the ground, leaving in its place all the lumber scraps and bricks and other trash to be hauled off at someone else's convenience. She was sitting in what had once been the bathroom, looking up at the open sky. And amazingly it was clearing. In the wake of what had blown through, a little patch of sun was beginning to peek out of the clouds.

"Danica," Cameron shouted.

His voice jolted her out of the shock of seeing the carnage surrounding her. "Are you injured? Where are you?"

"I'm under a wall, don't know where it is."

"Don't move. Do you understand me, Cameron? *Do not move.* I've got to make sure everything is secured before we try and get you out." Tom wouldn't have listened to her. Cameron would. She was sure of it.

"Understood," he called back. "And you be careful. I don't want you taking any risks."

Dag! She needed Dag! Her heart clutched at the thought. She didn't care about her house, but she'd left Dag shut inside. "Just talk to me, Cameron," she yelled, trying to push her worry for Dag from her mind. And her worry for Robby.

As she stood up, she looked down the street, and on this side none of the buildings were standing. On the other there were a few partial walls, nothing complete. And so far no survivors poking out of the wreckage. Not a good sign.

Cars were upturned everywhere, some blown into the places there'd once been buildings. A fairly large tugboat from the river was sitting in the middle of Main Street like it belonged there. It didn't appear to be damaged. Just out of place. And on both sides of the street, the streetlamps were curled over like wilting tulip stems. She saw a refrigerator sitting upside down on the curb, an empty wheelchair turned on its side, its wheels still spinning, and directly across the street in the place where the hardware store had been she saw what she believed was Cameron's roof. It was intact, just lifted across the street and set right back down, looking like it was waiting for the rest of the building to catch up with it.

She looked down toward the bakery. The building was still standing but there was so much debris all around it she couldn't tell what shape it was in. Robby and the others were safe in Nora's basement. *They had to be.* That's the only way she could think of it right now. They were together, helping each other get through this, and safe. They might be trapped under some of the bakery that had collapsed, but it would just be a matter of digging them out. That's all. Or maybe they were so busy eating Nora's pastries they hadn't noticed they could come out. She took another quick look then spun back around to the mess directly around her. "Talk to me, Cameron!"

"One thing's for sure. I hate your weather here."

It was so good to hear his voice sounding strong that, in spite of everything, she smiled. "So do I," she shouted, climbing her way over the piles of rubble to find him. She found him not far away, under what had been an exam room. True to her instructions, he hadn't budged, hadn't even begun to throw off the wall boards and drawers from his files cabinets that were pinning him down. "So how did you get moved?" Dropping to her knees, Dani began to push aside what she could, and throw off everything else until she finally saw his face.

With dirty face, and a cut ranging halfway across his forehead, he smiled up at her. And her heart melted. This was a man she would love for ever.

"Think I might have flown, but I'm not sure. One moment I was one place then suddenly I was someplace else." He wriggled his shoulder and arms free, then pushed himself up to a sitting position as she cleared the rest of the bits and pieces off him. "Are you OK?" he asked, rolling to one side to finally get completely clear. When he'd succeeded, he rolled back over and immediately pulled Dani into his arms. "Are you OK, Danica?" he asked, pulling her head to his chest.

She listened to his heart beating for a moment. A very nice heart. Steady. Strong. "I'm fine," she whispered. "I was afraid you'd…"

He chuckled. "To be honest, I was a little afraid of the same thing when I realized what was happening to me." Then his voice went serious. "And I was so afraid for you, that being there alone like that, something might have—" He bit off his words when his voice went thick.

"It's bad out there, Cameron. People are going to need help. I haven't seen anybody…and there's nothing left. The build-ings…gone. Robby… Dag…" Dani bit her quivering lip to stop the tears from starting. Then she straightened her shoulder and pushed away from Cameron. It would have been so easy staying there, clinging to him. But she couldn't. *They couldn't.* "I've got to…to…" The tears started anyway, and she swiped angrily at them as they trickled down her cheeks. "I've got to go help. Find survivors, set up a rescue grid…call my, um…my people." Global Response. She needed them here. All of them. Gideon and Lorna. Jason and Priscilla. Gwen. "I have to go to work, Cameron." From Texas to Indiana, they would be here in just a few hours, and she counted on that. *Counted on them.*

"Are you sure? Are you sure you can do this, Danica?"

She nodded with an air of confidence. "I can," she whis-pered. "I really can."

"Then what can I do to help you?"

"First find Robby. I have to know he's safe! Then we've got to go see…about Dag. It's going to be us for a while. No one else to help. We have to…do it all." And there was so much to do. "I've got to go." She stood first, then offered her hand to him, and as she pulled him up he went immediately into her arms, and for the shortest of moments she thought they were going to kiss. He tilted his face down to hers and came so close she could feel his breath on her. She even closed her eyes in the sweet anticipation because if ever there was a time she desperately needed to be kissed it was now. Then she waited…

"I can't!" he snapped, backing away from her.

She blinked her eyes wide open. She'd finally learned to love again, then this? "Why not?"

"We can't get involved. I can't get involved with you."

"Because I can't have children?" She had considered that, actually. Many times over the months she'd wondered what would happen if she risked a serious relationship again. Would the man she loved accept that she could never give him children? Well, apparently she had her answer now.

Stricken, she backed away.

"Children? Oh, my God, no, Danica! That's not it. I wouldn't… I couldn't…" He paused for a moment, then drew in a deep breath. "I can't get involved with you because I have cancer. Leukemia."

CHAPTER TEN

"He's asleep?" Danica asked.

Nora smiled. "Once he figured out that I was the lady with the treats, he settled right down. He ate a couple sugar cakes then went right off to sleep."

Dani brushed a strand of hair back from Robby's face as she looked up and down the street for Cameron. He'd checked to make sure Robby was unhurt, then he'd gone and she didn't know where. "The innocence of a child," she said, leaning over to kiss him on the cheek.

"You do what you have to do, Dani. You know he'll be safe with me, and the town needs you."

"I want to keep him," she confessed to her friend.

"You'll be a good mother," Nora said, then headed back to the stairs into the basement. She'd set up a temporary bed down there for Robby and now it was time to put him back.

Dani climbed through the piles of debris in the bakery and made it back to the street, where a large group had assembled, all awaiting her instructions. Greg LeMasters, the sheriff, was telling everybody she was in charge for now, and these people simply trusted that to be true, and trusted that she knew what to do.

She took a deep breath. This was what she did, a large part of who she was. It was time to reclaim that part of her life. "We need chainsaws and shovels," she shouted. It had been half an hour since she'd crawled out of the debris, a little less since Cameron's shocking pronouncement of leukemia, and now people were finding their way out of their own piles of rubble to gather in what used to be the center of town. "Pry tools, sledgehammers, and I need a couple of volunteers to go over to the clinic and see if you can find any medical supplies. We'll also need water. I want some of you to go to what's left of the grocery store and see if you can find bottled water…anything that is drinkable." Tap water wouldn't do. So often, in disasters such as this, the water supply was contaminated.

People responded very quickly. They listened to her directions, then acted. No hesitation, no doubt. But they couldn't see all the hesitation and doubt in her, and it was there, just not taking over the urgent need to act. Of course, she was hanging onto Gideon Merrill's assurance that he and Global Response were *en route*. Her friends. The people she loved. The people she worked with. A quick call had mobilized them almost immediately.

There had been little word from any of the nearby towns except that there was more damage down the river. Which meant other outside resources would be stretched thin, if there were any to be had. So for now the group of twenty or so people standing in front of her, waiting to be told what to do, was all she had.

"You're going to start your searching in pairs. Never, ever go out on your own. Don't separate, don't get outside each other's sight. If someone needs to be rescued and you can do it easily, without dislodging debris, do it. If they're injured badly, call me first. If you need to remove anything on top of them, or if there's a risk that something else could dislodge and come down on them, or you, call me! No exceptions! And if you have any doubts about anything, call me." She didn't have a two-way radio like she was used to, and cell phones weren't working. Which meant the old-fashioned way would have to do—a voice relay from one person to the next. "Shout it out to the person next to you and they will shout it out to the next person on down, and so on, until it reaches me. Right now it's about getting to the people as quickly as we can, so don't pull out personal belongings even if someone begs you to." She made quick assignments that sent the people in various directions. In lieu of an organized rescue grid, they would start searching at the center of town and work out from there.

She wished Cameron was here. She needed to set up an emergency center in one of the standing buildings. Probably the bank, as it looked to be the least damaged place on Main Street. He should be the one to handle the incoming patients while she ran the field operation. Maybe he was nearby and she couldn't see him. But she'd looked for him over and over these last minutes, and nothing. So there was nothing to do but get the field operation going and hope the rest would fall into place.

The field operation… Dani turned in a circle, simply staring at all the destruction around her. Out in the field, when Global Response went to a site like this, she'd always looked but had never truly seen so much. Now every detail hit her hard. This was personal, the people needing rescue were her friends. There was so much to do with so little. And she desperately needed Cameron, and not just for his medical skills. He was the substance of her emotional balance, the support she needed. The man she loved, cancer or not. Even thinking about that brought a lump to her throat. She'd wondered what it was that kept him so secretive and at a distance. Now she knew. And it hurt her deeply. "Keep in touch. Stay together. Be careful, and good luck," she shouted after them as the last of her workers went out.

After all her volunteers had dispersed, Dani stood there another minute, still trying to figure out where to begin. "An emergency center," she whispered, flagging Greg LeMasters over to her as she headed toward the bank. "Have you been out of town yet?" she asked. "In the outlying areas or any of the country roads?"

"Not very far, but I've got a couple men out there and they've said it hit some of the outermost areas pretty hard. Houses down, no word on casualties."

She thought about Dag for a minute. "Were you out my way?"

He shook his head. "Trees and electrical wires down near your house. Couldn't get through, and I had one of my men cordon off the road until we can get the power turned off and the wires moved. Sorry."

Dani swallowed hard, and nodded. "Have you called anybody for help?"

"State police, state disaster response. They know we need help, but we're not the only ones. They said they'd do their best to get through to us, but I don't think that's going to be for a while."

Just as she'd expected. "OK, well, the first thing I'm going to need is for you to get me inside the bank. I'm sure it's locked. And the second thing will be as many blankets and pillows as we can round up. From anywhere. Also, maybe when you go back out you'll find some others who can help us."

"Will do, Dani. And where's the doc, by the way? He didn't…?" He cut himself short and his face blanched.

"He's fine. I think he's out making an assessment." He wouldn't run away from this. Run away from her, yes, but not from a town needing so much help. In her heart she knew Cameron was out there somewhere, helping.

Greg used a master key to let her into the bank—he had a master for every building in town—then left her there to return to what everybody else was doing—searching.

Before Dani stepped inside, she looked up and down the street one more time for Cameron, then resigned herself to the fact that he was probably avoiding her. She'd been quite plain about what she'd wanted, even if it was only a kiss. And he'd been quite plain about what he didn't want. Which was her on any terms other than as an acquaintance. One at an arm's length, at that.

"OK, so I'm not her, but I'm doing the best I can." Cameron was leading Dag across a field, trying to get back to town. Danica's house had taken a hit, lost some roof and windows, but nothing substantial compared to what so many others had lost. He'd gone for Dag because he was dispensable in town, she was not. And she would need her dog to do her job.

"Damn," he muttered, stepping over a small tree trunk. "I should have done it better. Hey, Danica, I can't kiss you because I've got cancer." He cringed, thinking about it. "I wanted to kiss her, Dag. Hell, I've wanted to kiss her from the first time I saw her." In his past, he would have. No big deal then. But it was now. His future wasn't certain, and he wasn't about to drag someone into it. Especially not Danica. She'd already lost one boyfriend. No way was he going to pull her in even close to that again. She didn't deserve it, and he cared far too much for her to put her through all those doubts and fears like he'd had for the past three years. Cancer was the nightmare that didn't go away even after it was cured. It took so long, called on so many emotions, and he wouldn't involve her in that, no matter how he felt about her. And he did love her.

"But I'm not going to get involved with anything more than I already have in my life. Not until I have all of my life back," he told the dog. "Whatever that's going to be." Admittedly, that was some of the concern, because he didn't know what he wanted. Go back to Boston, to his old practice…to Sarah? She wasn't waiting for him, but the fact that she'd been one of his partners would put them back into contact, and how could that ever be a good working situation? He did want to be considerate with her about that. It was the very least he owed her. "And let me tell you, Dag, there are some bridges, once you've burned them down, that you should never try to build back up."

Then there was the fact that he wasn't sure he wanted that pace of life any more. Coming close to death as he'd done, had a way of changing outlooks and perspectives. His *had* been changed but he wasn't sure yet if he was still in transition or if he'd reached the place he wanted to be. Sometimes if felt like he had. But at other times he just felt empty. In a struggle like Danica's, uncertainty was the enemy. It was a paralyzing effect that stopped you from progressing, and she had enough of that on her own right now, without getting the fallout from his leftovers. Then if she did with Robby what he thought she might…

"So, the bottom line is, I don't know," he said to the dog. "And as long as I don't know where I'm going, I'm not going to drag along any emotional involvements."

Unfortunately, he'd have to put away the feelings he'd developed for Danica, like he'd done with the symptoms of his illness. *More denial.* Except, in a manner of speaking, his leukemia had been cured. Or, at least, put into remission. His feelings for Danica never would, and he wouldn't deny it.

And as for Robby…he *would* do right there. He wanted to, and it was about more than his obligation as Robby's doctor. Something about the child drew him in and compelled him to help. For no reason that made good sense to him, he knew, deep inside, that Danica was the one who was supposed to take care of Robby. He'd known it the night she'd found him, known it that day in the hospital when he'd watched her sit and rock him. And, yes, he wanted to be a part of that, but neither Danica nor Robby needed the instability of his cancer in their lives. They'd both suffered such hard losses already. In case his cancer returned, it was better to spare them yet another loss.

They would have each other, but sadly he would have neither of them. That's the hand fate had dealt him, though, and this time he was going to make sure he played it the right way, for their sakes.

"I'm going to put makeshift beds on the floor," she explained to Lena Harmon, the woman who owned the beauty shop. The shop had been flattened. All that was left was one chair sitting in its normal spot. Everything else around it was gone. But Lena and several of her patrons were lined up at the bank ready to work, in spite of their losses.

"I've got people out looking for supplies now, and when they bring them back, I need you to arrange them, get the place fit for patients."

"Don't you worry," Lena said cheerfully, like she hadn't lost everything she owned in this world. "When they bring them in here, I'll make sure everything is taken care of." She gave Dani's hand a squeeze. "And I'm so glad you're feeling better. With you here to get us through…" She sniffled, then smiled. "You take care of yourself and as soon as I get my shop set back up, you've got free hair care for the rest of your life!"

Dani returned the smile. In the midst of all the loss, there was no question that the people in this little town would make it. They were resilient.

"Dani!" someone shouted from the front of the bank building. "Got an injury."

The first of many to come, she guessed.

Two men carried the first person in and sat him gently down on the marble floor. Dani dropped to her knees to do a quick assessment without any medical equipment, and started with the man's face. He was conscious, his eyes barely opened, and he was a mass of tiny cuts. Glass shards, she guessed. Lots of blood, nothing serious. "Any in your eyes?" she asked him.

"Not that I know of," he forced out, trying not to contort his face too much. "Doesn't feel like it."

She pulled up his shirt, and saw the same kinds of injuries, mostly cuts. The same for his back. But his leg…the gash on his right calf was deep, almost to the bone. Someone had wrapped it in a bath towel and it had bled through. The man was losing a tremendous amount of blood and there was nothing to do for him but apply pressure and wait. She called over one of Lena's beauty-salon ladies to do just that, then scrambled to the front door to greet another patient coming in. Two more entered almost immediately, followed by another. And so it began. She took a deep breath, thought briefly about the men she loved— big and small—and began to assess the various wounds.

"I've sent a couple of your volunteers out to pillage your house for anything we can use here," Cameron said from behind Dani, as she assessed an elderly man's head wound for bandaging.

She spun around, right into Cameron. "What…?" She looked down and saw Dag. "You went to get him?"

"I thought you might be needing him."

She wasn't sure whether to laugh or cry. Or kiss Cameron, even though she knew he wouldn't want that. "They said the wires are down out there."

"All over the road."

"Then how?"

He grinned at her. "A long walk through the meadow, and let me say that your partner here is none too co-operative with a stranger. But I thought it was important to get him to you."

Dani dropped to her knees to hug Dag, even though she'd rather have been hugging Cameron. "I thought you were avoiding me," she said. "When you walked away…"

"I was. Probably will be again once this thing is over."

"And just when I was about to tell you that I love you."

"Don't do that, Danica," he warned, his voice so serious it was distorted. "You're wasting your time because I'm not getting involved."

"Telling someone you love them is never a waste of time. Trust me, I've learned that the hard way. I don't even remember saying it to Tom. I know I must have, but right now I don't remember. And if something were to happen now…" She swallowed back a big lump. "I want to say it enough so I'll remember. I love you, Cameron. Like it or not, and accept it or not, I love you." She stood back up and took Dag's lead from Cameron's hand. "You have patients coming in, Doctor. Head wound here, possible broken arm there, a deep leg gash with substantial blood loss." She pointed out the various patients. "Now I'll leave you in charge to do what you do best while I go out and do what I do." Dani started to walk away, then turned back to him. "And in case you didn't hear me the first time, I do love you, Cameron Enderlein. You may not want to hear it but you're going to be hearing it again, every chance I get."

As Dani's rubber-soled walking shoes squeaked across the marble floor on her way to the front door, a smile crept across her lips. He may have said he wasn't getting involved but he was already involved. And Dr. Cameron Enderlein definitely wasn't a waste of her time.

"Dani!"

She spun around to see Gideon Merrill running toward her. It was so good to see him again. She'd worked so many mission with him, but since the accident she'd thought that was in the past. "Gideon!" she cried, running into his arms.

"How are you?" he asked.

"Good. Really good." She glanced across the street at the bank, aching to go over there to see how Cameron was doing. She was worried. The casualties were coming in one by one, and they were everywhere now. Some badly injured, some superficially. Cameron was the only medic at work, and he was still being assisted by Lena and several of her patrons. A meager assortment of supplies had been pulled in from his office, but not enough to make much of a difference. "Tired, but physically I'm so much better now."

"We got here as fast as we could. It wasn't easy getting clearance to land, which is why it took us longer than we'd originally anticipated."

"Doesn't matter. You're here, and we need you." She pointed to the bank. "Temporary hospital. Few supplies. That's the first priority because I've only got one trained medic in there." Then she pointed to the post office. "I've set up the command post in there. And over there…" The library. "I've got people bringing in all the usable supplies they can find and turning that into a storehouse."

"Good work," he said, turning in a circle to look at the carnage. "What kind of casualties?"

"Don't have a count yet. But there are a lot of them. Some serious, a lot with superficial injuries. Dag and I have been out looking for the past couple of hours, rescued about a dozen people, and so far no fatalities." She glanced over at Lorna, Gideon's wife. She had her dog, Maisey, with her. And Priscilla, who was married to Gideon's partner Jason, had Philo on his leash, raring to get out on the search. Suddenly, she ached for all she'd missed with them. And she was sad not to see Tom there. But that ache was changing. What Cameron had said about cherishing the memories… She was now. Finally, she was able to do that.

"When we flew over, it looked like it extends for several miles," Gideon said.

"I'm not surprised. Look, I need to go check on someone. How many other doctors came down?"

"All of them, Dani. All seven of us. Nine nurses, five paramedics, six rescue volunteers."

She was stunned, almost to tears. "We don't have supplies…"

"We do," he said, pulling her back into his arms. "And we're going to take care of you. We're going to take care of everybody."

"You always have. You, Lorna, Jason and Priscilla."

"We're family, Dani. That's what family does."

They *were* family. And all these months through her recovery, that was one thing she hadn't doubted. "I'm sorry I was so mean to you there for a while before I came home."

He clicked on his two-way radio. "Medical operation to the bank building, everybody else to the post office." Then he clicked off and gave her a wink. "You look like you could use two hours off for a rest. Rules, you know."

Gideon's standard protocol. Work six hours, rest for two. Some things never changed. Thank God.

"Time for a break," Dani told Cameron. He was kneeling on the floor, bandaging an elderly man's broken hand.

He looked up at her, his expression telling her she must be crazy to call him off in the middle of all this.

"We have doctors and nurses and paramedics," she continued. "And supplies." She pointed to the door where the rescue workers were trooping in one at a time, each carrying a box of medical equipment. "It's Gideon's operation now. I've turned it over to him, and the rule is you've got to take a two-hour break. No exceptions."

"And this is where I should argue with you and tell you I don't work for Gideon," he said, standing up. "Except I'm too damned tired, my back and knees are killing me, and I need that two hours."

"So do I," she whispered, then held out her hand to him. "Want to take your break with me?"

"Look, Danica, I already told you—"

"I don't have my quilt," she said, her hand still outstretched.

"What?"

"My pity quilt. The one I hide under when I don't want to be bothered. I believe it's covering that woman over there." She pointed to a woman bedded down on the floor who was, indeed, covered by the quilt. It had been gathered up with other bedding during a raid on all the standing houses in town. "Otherwise I'd give it to you."

"What you said earlier, about loving me…"

She didn't wait for him to finish. She grabbed hold of his arm as he wouldn't hold her hand, and she, Cameron and Dag went to the bank president's office and shut the door. "It's time to rest," she said. "And you're not looking so good."

"So now you're going to start fussing over me? That's exactly the reason why I'd decided not to tell people about my condition."

The floor in the office was carpeted, and she slid down, and kept on sliding until she was on her back. "It was fine when you wanted to fuss over me, but let me mention one little thing—that you're not looking so good—and now you're angry. Well, be angry. Just do it quietly, OK?" With that she shut her eyes.

"I have good reasons," he continued.

"I'm sure you do."

"I haven't hit my five-year mark yet. My oncologist thinks that a five-year remission is what it'll take to pronounce me cured, and I've got a long way to go to get there."

"OK, then I'll quit loving you. When you reach that anniversary, though, will you ring me up and let me know so I can start loving you again?" She opened her eyes a crack to look up at him, and found him standing directly over her, staring down. "What now?"

"I heard so many things about you before you got here—one being that you were stubborn."

"And persistent," she added.

He laughed. "And infuriating."

"I don't care about your cancer, you know. Were you bald?"

He nodded, and finally sank down to the carpet next to her. "Totally."

"Could have been a nice look. Bald's popular now." She smiled, wrinkling her nose. "I could get used to it on you."

"You can disarm me, Danica, and you're doing a damn fine job of it, but that won't change things between us. I'm not getting involved with you."

"You mean you're not getting involved more than you already are?" She snuggled into his side as he stretched flat out. "Because you're the one who started this, back when I was the one who didn't want to get involved."

"When I wanted to be your friend. *Only* your friend."

"And you don't now?"

He didn't answer.

"One thing I've learned, Cameron, is that life's short. We don't really get so much time here and if you're lucky enough to love someone along the way, you have to tell them because there are no guarantees. You and I both know that in ways most people don't realize. If you love someone right now, tell them right now because this may be the only moment you have. And how sad would it be to never tell someone that you love them because you think you'll always have tomorrow, but when tomorrow comes you've lost that opportunity for ever? Well, I won't do that and, whether or not you want to hear it, I do love you."

No answer again, but he wasn't sleeping. His breathing wasn't deep enough.

It would have been nice thinking that he was planning on a way to tell her that he loved her, but somehow she doubted that was the case. More like he was plotting a way to get away from her.

Even so, she was glad she'd told him.

Dani tucked her head against his upper arm, shut her eyes, and sighed. Being in love was nice. Being in love with someone who loved her back would be nicer. Either way, this was *the moment* and there might not be another one. She had no regrets.

How could she stay there like that, all curled up against him, sleeping? He'd tried to do the same, but so far all he'd succeeded in doing was getting a stiff arm where her head was resting on him. Thinking. Thinking more.

It was crazy. He couldn't have feelings for her. There were too many pitfalls for both of them. Especially for her. Yet there she was, as brave as anyone he'd ever known in his life, telling him she loved him, even though she knew he was going to reject her. Telling him, then telling him again. And she knew now! Leukemia in remission didn't necessarily mean leukemia cured, and yet she dared say those words to him.

Cameron shifted Dani's weight off his arm, rolled away from her then stood up. He crossed the room to the window and looked outside to all the activity there. People were coming and going in every direction…all of them involved in the aftermath of a huge tragedy. Some were helping others, some were clearing debris…it was an amazing scene. One like he'd never witnessed in his life. There was such strength out there. Just this morning they had all woken up like they did every other day, had had their coffee, taken a shower and set about life as normal. Then, suddenly, everything they'd known as normal had been ripped away from them, the way his leukemia had ripped everything away from him, and the way a mudslide in Brazil had ripped everything away from Danica.

Yet here were these people, knocked down and getting back up. Nothing keeping them down. And no guarantees that what they put back together today would be here tomorrow.

"It's overwhelming," she said, slipping up quietly behind him and wrapping her arms around his waist.

He liked the feeling. Liked everything about the way she

pressed herself so naturally up against him. He'd had relationships in the past, a few casual ones, a couple of near hits… Sarah. But none had ever felt like this. Danica felt like…home, and for ever and the only place he ever wanted to be. And here she was, giving herself to him after all she'd been through, yet he wasn't taking what he desperately wanted. He was afraid…not of the cancer, not even of death. He was afraid of loving Danica the way he knew he did. She needed more than the uncertainties, more than the ups and downs, and he would have them. That was a given. Catching a normal cold or having an ache and pain like everyone did from time to time was different for someone recovering from cancer because everything made them think their cancer was coming back. No matter what, the old fears always resurfaced.

There were anxieties over the required tests, and he would have to have so many tests over the next years. Then the waiting period for the test results…he was always grumpy during that time. Everyone awaiting those results got grumpy. And physical limitations…he had them. It was all a vicious cycle of emotions for a long time, and one that was easier to go through alone because, perhaps, his greatest fear of all was anticipating the look on her face the day she grew tired of enduring those cycles with him. She would try hiding it, of course. Danica was that way. But he would see it in her eyes, and it would break his heart that he was cheating her of the life she deserved. The way he had cheated Sarah by letting her hang on.

So this was where he had to end it, even though it had never really started. "It *is* overwhelming," he agreed.

"But people struggle back. That's all you can do."

"You're talking from personal experience."

"Some. But I've seen recovery in so many forms, and I'm always amazed. For some people, like me, it takes a while. Others, though, just get up and it starts. Like Helen Robertson there." She pointed to the gray-haired octogenarian scurrying down the street with an armload of blankets. "She lived in the apartment above the hardware store and her home is gone now, yet she's in there with everybody else, doing everything she can to help. She knows she has no place to go tonight, but she's not sitting on the curb crying about it."

"Maybe it's avoidance."

"Or maybe it's a passion to squeeze every drop out of life no matter what life hands her. I missed a lot of time, Cameron. After all my surgeries, I had months and months of physical recovery, but when I was well on the mend from that, I certainly was no Helen Robertson, getting on with life the way she is. I knew I needed to. Intellectually, I was trying, but I needed a push, and you're the one who gave it to me. It would be nice to think I could have gotten over it on my own, but I did need your help. We all need help sometimes, and that's a lesson you've taught me."

"I helped you and now you think you have to pay me back? You're…obligated?" The way Sarah had felt obligated. "Is that it? You're feeling obligated to help me get through, to push me back into life? Because I don't need that, Danica. I'm working, I'm functioning."

"It's not an obligation, Cameron. Not when it's something you want to do. And maybe you're working and functioning, but you're also avoiding."

"Avoiding a relationship with you. That's all."

"Do you love me, Cameron?"

Of course he did. Which was why he wouldn't do this.

"Do you love me?" she asked again. "All I need is a simple yes or no. Even nodding or shaking your head will be fine."

"My feelings don't matter," he finally said.

"You know, a few hours ago, when the tornado tore down your office all around us, and I couldn't find you…I was so scared. And it wasn't because I'd gone through this before with

Tom. It was because I thought I'd lost *you*. What I was feeling for those few moments, until I heard your voice was about a life without you. *You, Cameron.* And cancer doesn't matter, and it doesn't change my feelings. I know what it is, I know what it does. And it doesn't matter."

He broke free from her hold and spun around. "You don't know, Danica!" he cried. "For the past three years I've lived day to day. That's all there is. I can't make plans for next year. Sure, I'm in a remission, but I've still got so far to go before I'm pronounced cured, and I can't set long-term goals."

"Why not?" she asked quite bluntly. Before he had a chance to answer, though, she continued. "When I was injured, I really thought I was going to die. I knew how serious it was, knew my odds. I wasn't even sure they would be able to transport me to a hospital, but I remember making plans to have a dance with Tom when I was better. That's what got me through those first hours until the doctors stabilized me. I didn't know he'd died, and all I did was make plans…dream. It gave me something to live for. Something to fight for. And for a while I really did have to fight to stay alive."

"But you never had that dance, did you, so what good were your plans?"

"They were my lifeline, Cameron. And, no, they didn't happen. But that's not the point. In the bad times we have to have something to look forward to in the good times or all we can see are the bad times. For me personally I needed those plans, had to have something in my future to look forward to. Without plans and ideas and dreams, we're already half-dead." She brushed away a tear sliding down her cheek. "And I don't want you half-dead, Cameron."

Dear God, he loved this woman. And here he was, standing so far away from her. Not in a literal sense, but in an emotional one. "I don't dance," he said.

She laughed, then sniffled. "Neither do I, really. I'm more of a toe-stepper. Get your toes in my way and they get stepped on. And I want to step on your toes, Cameron."

"Danica, I…" He shrugged, still fighting himself over this. For Danica's sake he should push her away. But all he wanted to do was pull her close. "When I was first diagnosed I was just weeks away from getting married. We postponed it, of course. Decided to wait until I was through the first round of treatment and not so sick. She was one of my partners at work. Sarah Collins. The woman I truly thought was the love of my life. And I suppose you could say that at the start of our relationship, she was. But I got sick, and trust me when I tell you that the first course of my illness wasn't easy…not for either of us. I got weaker, refused to quit work. Went on chemo. Had every one of the bad side-effects you can imagine, and Sarah stayed with me. She felt obligated, and I let her.

"But the look on her face over the months…it went from love and concern to revulsion. Oh, she tried to hide it. But she was like you. Everything was right there, in her eyes. She couldn't hide it. I do know she tried, but it was so difficult for her. Cancer takes its toll in so many ways…"

"Did she leave you?"

"Actually, no. She stayed for a while, and there were many times I'd hear her crying in her room…we quit sleeping in the same room after the first month. And she wasn't crying for me, Danica. She wanted out, but she felt trapped because she thought that walking away from someone with cancer would make her a monster. Which she wasn't. Sarah was merely someone who couldn't cope with what I was going through, and I never held that against her. Finally, I was the one who left her—because I loved her and she deserved the kind of life she couldn't have with me. She's getting happy again. And if I'd have insisted, she'd have married me, which would have ruined her life."

"You let her go because you loved her?"

"She had to go."

"But she loved you?"

He sighed, then nodded. "Sometimes there's just not enough to make it work no matter how hard you try, and Sarah did try."

"But sometimes there is," she said gently. "Sarah made her choice because she was already with you when you were diagnosed and she felt an obligation to do that. Most people would, I think. But I'm not with you, Cameron. You've never let me close and you've done everything you could to keep me at a distance. And guess what? Even though I know about your leukemia, I still want to be with you, even though you make it easy for me not to choose that. But I don't want to. And in case you haven't noticed, I'm the one who's standing here putting my heart on the line, telling you I love you when there's every good chance you'll reject me. I'm so sorry about your cancer, Cameron, and I'm sorry about the fears that Sarah has caused in you and the doubts your relationship with her have raised. But that doesn't change my feelings for you. Not even a little. I want to be with you and I want to stay."

"But we've got to face facts, Danica. What if the leukemia comes back? You lost Tom. I don't want you to have to go through that again, and it could happen. And do I really have the right to ask you to face that possibility? I know that deep down you think you can, but you've been there before, and so recently, and what would it do to you if I died?" Frustrated, he shook his head. "If I hadn't had leukemia, I wouldn't have all these concerns…"

"And if you hadn't had leukemia, you wouldn't have had what I needed to get me through my own accident, Cameron. Don't you see that? What you did for me is because of who you've become. Someone who hasn't suffered in a profoundly tragic way can sympathize, but they can't truly understand. And you understood…understood what I needed even when I didn't."

"So it gives me deeper insight, but along with the insight I have a pretty damned clear vision of me dragging you down like I did Sarah, and I don't want to do that, Danica. I can't."

"Can you walk away from me, Cameron? Honestly, can you turn your back, walk out that door and never look back?"

He squared his shoulders. "Yes," he said, his voice curt. "If I have to."

"Can you do that to Robby? I mean, what about him? Why were you so compelled to take him in? I know you didn't want him in an institution, but what else? And what was it, Cameron, that made you keep coming back to my house all those mornings, even when I didn't want you there, and forced you to take Robby in when you're not really set up to take care of a child?" Her voice softened. "Why is it that you wanted to help us…help me…but yet you're pushing me away?"

"I've learned so many things about myself. Good things, bad things. When you think you're going to die, it suddenly becomes important to do a lot of soul-searching. You find this deep need to put things right."

"I did it, too," she said.

"Well, what I did was…wrong. I used my cancer to keep Sarah around because I didn't want to be alone. And I used my cancer to keep working when I should have gone on leave. I blackmailed people with it because—"

"Because you were scared," Dani interrupted.

"Because I was being a selfish bastard. It was my problem, nobody else's, yet I forced them to deal with it. Hung onto my girlfriend, forced myself on my partners…"

"You weren't being selfish, Cameron. You were just avoiding the obvious. We all do it in our own ways. You did what you did to keep people around, and I hid under my quilt to keep them away. That's what you saw in me because that's what you knew you had in you. And it's what you know Robby will have to deal with, which is why you took him. You have the deep, abiding need to help those around you."

"I didn't help Sarah."

"But that's in the past. You were the one who left her, weren't you? And couldn't your partners have forced you to take a leave if you'd really become a problem to the medical practice? Surely they would have, and you know what, Cameron? I don't think there are any clear-cut answers here. No real rights or wrongs. You feel guilty because Sarah stayed and was miserable, and you let her. But what would her guilt over leaving you at that point in your illness have done to her? Have you ever thought about that? I think you both shut off from each other, and at the time you were probably handling it the only way you could. Like I said, there aren't any clear answers because these are the kinds of things no one gets any practice for in life. They happen and you're forced to accept them for what they are and move on. It's the best any of us can do, and, yes, we make mistakes. You and Sarah did by not communicating your feelings to each other, I did by running from place to place to place every time someone tried to get close to me. We all do when we're faced with extraordinary situations. But that doesn't make us bad. It makes us…human, inexperienced."

She laid her hand over Cameron's heart. "I don't want to be pushed away from you, Cameron. What you have in there is so good and compassionate and strong. I do know the facts about leukemia but I don't pity you, and I think that's what you fear the most, isn't it? That someone will stay with you out of pity? That Sarah stayed out of pity, that your partners kept you on out of pity. That I'll make this grand play for you then stand by your side because I pity you. But I won't, Cameron, because I know what it's like to not want to be pitied. More than anybody else, I do know that. It's why I came here to Lexington, to hide from the pity and find my own strength on my own, and I promise I don't pity you. *I won't pity you.* But I'll support you, which is entirely different."

"Sometimes it *is* easier to do it on your own," he said.

"To every season there's a time," she said, "and there is a season when it's nice to have someone to help. And you taught me that, Cameron. Intellectually, I knew it, but you're the one who showed me how. Life doesn't come with a road map, not for any of us. I really believe, though, that with two of us fighting for you, instead of you doing it all alone, your leukemia wouldn't dare come back. And if we get to adopt Robby…"

"Adopt him?"

She nodded, smiling. "I was actually on my way to talk to you about it this morning when the tornado struck. I've decided to try for adoption. He needs us. We need him, too. And better than anyone else, we know the battles ahead of him. You knew that when you took him in. You knew that we had to be the ones to help him. Not to pity him but to give him everything you've given me and everything I want to give you."

"That almost sounds like a marriage proposal for three."

"It does, doesn't it?" she said, smiling. "So, what's the answer?"

"You *are* persistent."

"Persistently in love."

The three of them…that was a fine plan for the future. He wasn't sure how it would work out, but Danica was right about one thing, that even thinking he could have all that gave him a hope he hadn't felt in a long, long time. "I love you," he whispered. "Just as long as you understand…"

She didn't let him finish. And he didn't want to as she wrapped her arms around his neck and pulled his face to hers. "Do you want to kiss me now?" she asked.

His answer was sealed on her lips.

EPILOGUE

EPILOGUE

"NOT bad," Danica said, stepping into Cameron's waiting room. It was larger than the old one. Had much more of a permanent feel to it now. She'd helped him with the decorating, and had even acted as his office nurse for a while since he'd been practicing medicine in the parlor of her house in lieu of a real office. Mostly, though, she'd been spending her time with Robby, being the full-time mother he needed during the rough months of his adjustment, and being the full-time mother she needed to be.

It had been a perfect situation, the three of them healing each other, and, truly, it had taken all three to get them to this point. Three people who had lost so much then found so much in each other.

Cameron and Robby had come down early that morning, and Robby was eagerly trying out all the new toys in the children's corner. At the moment, he was busy with a toy train, but as Dani stepped in he did look up briefly and smile. "Hi, Mama!" he squealed, the way only a happy, excited child could, as he held up his toy for her to see.

Every time he called her *Mama* her heart just melted. Technically, she wasn't yet. But soon. It was in the works, and now she and Cameron were waiting. In fact, with Christmas just weeks off, it was her fondest wish to be Robby's real mother for the holidays. "Hi, sweetheart. Are you having fun?"

He gave her a vigorous nod then went right back to playing with the train.

"You know he wants a set of his own for Christmas," Cameron said, stepping out of the back room and immediately pulling Dani into his arms.

He was so handsome, standing there in his white lab coat. He'd finally given up his practice in Boston, sold his share to his partners, and invested in building a much nicer office in Lexington. One with an adjoining office for the new town veterinarian. "He wants a lot of things," she said, pulling the list from her pocket. Then she stood on tiptoe and whispered, "And I can't wait to buy every last one of them, Dr. Enderlein."

"You'll spoil him, Dr. Enderlein."

"I like spoiling my men."

Cameron bent his head and kissed her. Since that first kiss he'd never turned her down. "Care to see my exam room?" he asked afterwards, with a wicked arch to his eyebrows.

She laughed. "You're incorrigible."

"I'm happy." He pulled a slip of paper from his pocket and handed it to her. "Completely normal. Everything." He was referring to his latest round of blood tests. They were much less frequent these days. In fact, the oncologist had pronounced his remission as a *cure* just a few weeks ago, much ahead of the time they'd expected, and Cameron's follow-up appointments and tests had gone from maintenance to merely routine. In other words, Cameron's doctor was fairly sure the cancer would not return. In her heart, Dani knew her beloved husband had beaten his cancer all the way.

Instead of looking at the test results, Dani balled up the paper and tossed it into the trash. "Maybe we should take Robby over to my grandmother's for the night and have a celebration." They celebrated every good test result, and so far all of them had been good.

"Brilliant idea." He gave her a little nudge toward the door. "Maybe we should leave right away. Why don't you go pack him a few clothes…?"

"Just a minute," she said, resisting his nudge. "I talked to Gideon today, and—"

"And he wants you to move back to Texas and go to work for them again?" A slight frown creased his face. "Isn't Texas awfully hot in the summer? I mean, I'm willing to move there with you, but I've got to find another doctor to take over here, and then I've…"

Smiling, Dani he raised a finger to his lips. "We won't be going to Texas, so you don't have to start making plans to move. Gideon wants me to start an operation here, one that will specialize in training rescue dogs. Open up a facility on our property, as there's so much of it that goes with the house. He's finally got some good funding coming in, and he and his partner believe it's time Global Response expanded. They want me to head this part of the operation, if I want it."

"Along with your veterinary practice? You'd be perfect!"

"I'll be busy, but as my veterinary practice is only going to be part time, I'll manage. But I will have to be gone occasionally, field training, some on-site rescue training. If I do that, then it means you and Robby…"

"We'll love you very much and miss you when you're gone. And it's not like half the women in town aren't dying to take care of him. As well as your grandmother…"

Robby *had* become quite the man in town for all her friends here…Nora, Lena and the beauty shop ladies… And as for her grandmother, even the slightest hint that she might get to care for her soon-to-be great-grandson brought her running, golf game, tennis game, or not. "Then you don't mind? Because I might have to go out with his Texas operation from time to time. Not often, but it might happen."

"Do I mind that you're following your heart? You did once, even though I was pushing you away, and it's the best thing that ever happened to me. So how could I ever stop you from having anything you want?"

"What I want is you, and Robby."

He laughed. "My Danica has many more plans than that. She always has, always will, which is one of the things I love most about her. She has room for so much in her life."

He still called her Danica, but it was intimately personal now, and she loved that. He was the only one who did, the only one she wanted to. "But you're happy?" He'd settled so nicely into town. They'd fixed up the Victorian house as the rest of the town was rebuilt, and over the months he'd taken on more medical duties. Now he was the town's full-time doctor and people didn't have to go over to Everly anymore. "And you're sure this isn't going to put a strain on us, because you're going to have to do everything for Robby when I'm gone?"

"Your boys are perfectly capable of taking care of themselves for a few days, even though they'll be glad to see you come home. And I'm very happy. This is the life I've always wanted." He took hold of her hand and pulled her along into his office. Then he pointed up to the spot between the door and the ceiling. An old rusty trombone was anchored to the wall there.

"Where'd you find it?"

"That day after the tornado struck and I'd gone to fetch Dag for you, it was just sitting in the pasture we had to come through. Propped up on an old wooden fence like it had always been there, waiting for me to come and take it home."

The way she'd been waiting for him to come and take *her* home. "What's that tucked in the bell of it?" she asked, pointing to a slip of paper sticking out.

"You'll have to look for yourself."

He had that look on his face, the mischievous one she'd come to love. There were so many things about Cameron she'd come to love, and the one thing that could be said for marrying a man she'd only known a month was that life was full of surprises. All good ones. In a sense, they'd both started with nothing, and in a short time they'd built so much. She still loved Tom, but not in the way she loved Cameron, and Cameron was fine with that. Just as she was fine that in some ways he still loved Sarah. Those parts of their lives had been what had brought them to this part of their lives, and for that, those memories would be a cherished part of the past. But they were making new memories now, and those would be the ones held most dear, forever.

"So I have to climb up there to get it?"

He pulled the chair over for her, and lent her a hand as she stepped up. Once she'd pulled out the paper, she read it right there. *The Court hereby decrees...*

By the time she'd read through to the last word she was sobbing so hard that Cameron pulled her down into his arms. "When?" she asked.

"About an hour ago. Dr. Wallace had it sent over a little while ago."

"So he's ours? Robby is our son?"

"Legally, emotionally, and in every other way, Robert Tilton Enderlein is our son."

"I'm a mother," she whispered though the tears. "I'm finally a mother. Should we go tell him?"

Cameron shook his head. "He's always known."

A family of her own. As her lips met her husband's, she realized she'd always known, too.

4 Books
and a surprise gift!

We would like to take this opportunity to thank you for reading this Mills & Boon® book by offering you the chance to take FOUR more specially selected titles from the Medical™ series absolutely FREE! We're also making this offer to introduce you to the benefits of the Mills & Boon® Reader Service™—

- ★ **FREE home delivery**
- ★ **FREE gifts and competitions**
- ★ **FREE monthly Newsletter**
- ★ **Exclusive Reader Service offers**
- ★ **Books available before they're in the shops**

Accepting these FREE books and gift places you under no obligation to buy, you may cancel at any time, even after receiving your free shipment. Simply complete your details below and return the entire page to the address below. You don't even need a stamp!

YES! Please send me 4 free Medical books and a surprise gift. I understand that unless you hear from me. I will receive 6 superb new titles every month for just £2.89 each. postage and packing free. I am under no obligation to purchase any books and may cancel my subscription at any time. The free books and gift will be mine to keep in any case.

M7ZEF

Ms/Mrs/Miss/Mr ....Initials...............................
Surname .... **BLOCK CAPITALS PLEASE**
Address...

....Postcode ....

Send this whole page to:
UK: FREEPOST CN81, Croydon, CR9 3WZ